Examining Christmas

An In-depth Look at the Nativity

Jason Lee Willis

Lura Publications

Mapleton, MN

Lura Publications
803 Silver Street E.
Mapleton, MN 56065
www.lurapublications.wixsite.com/books
williswrites.com

Book Layout © 2017 BookDesignTemplates.com

Examining the Christmas/ Jason Lee Willis. – 2nd ed.
ISBN: 979-8-9903790-7-7

For my 9:30 crew at Hosanna Lutheran.

I know when I'm amped up on coffee and the Holy Spirit, it is really hard to keep up with the notes, so hopefully this written account makes up for all of that frustration.

Contents

JUST A NERD WITH A BIBLE

I have no special talent, training, or certification other than I'm a curious fellow. This book you hold in your hand is far from infallible (or even professional), but it is my genuine purpose to leave a bit of myself behind. I received a Bible study book my grandfather read, and whenever I'd see something written down or underlined, it thrilled me to be able to peek inside of the mind of a man I hardly knew but who walked the same faith path. So this collection of Christmas research is my way to steal the spotlight during a future Willis Christmas with some "Hey, did you know…" moments.

Folks who have attended my Bible studies also know that I seek out the "biggest" and most "EPIC" interpretation I can find. I also do not have a specific denominational slant, and have often described myself as a "Luth-olic-a-tist," baptized Lutheran, a wannabe Catholic, a dabbler in Baptist, and the "a" can stand for whatever loose hair I have on a certain day. In other words, I'm much more "fisherman" than "Pharisee" in my training.

I've been accused of pondering things too long, which is why this study will not be an introduction to the Nativity story but more of a look outside of the box. I try to study each Biblical nugget from a variety of vantages just to see all the possibly meanings.

At worst, I hope this study will make you ponder your own interpretations of these awesome verses (old **KJV**) or do a little research on your own.

JLW

THE SCARLET THREAD

The Rotten Fig in the Family Tree

More than a thousand years before the fate of mankind would be determined in the little town of Bethlehem, two Hebrew men were faced with a decision that potentially doomed mankind.

These men were never named in the Book of Joshua, but the name of their condemned Canaanite prisoner lived on for thousands of years afterward. While the once-mighty city of Jericho burned, and the dying screams of its inhabitants filled the air, the two spies were faced with an ethical conundrum, a paradox of morality.

The Canaanites were the archenemies of the Hebrews, but not just because they possessed their lands and stood in their way following the exodus out of Egypt. The Canaanites had given themselves to the darkness, and foul gods such as Baal,

Anath, Molech, and Beelzebub hung on their dying breaths. The Promised Land had to be purged of this darkness—God had commanded it.

On the other hand, the two spies knew the face of the woman who wept at their feet. A short time earlier, she had not only given them shelter but she had also spared their lives when the King of Jericho came searching for the spies.

If not for her, both spies would have certainly been killed.

The sword of wrath was set aside.

The hand of mercy was extended, and not just to the woman, but to her entire family. Rahab the prostitute was spared.

So what does a prostitute have to do with Christmas?

Everything.

This is more than just a lesson about mercy and loving your enemies (neither of which is seen much in the Book of Joshua), this is all about understanding a single Canaanite's place in the context of history. As you follow the rest of this story, Joshua and the Hebrews go on to slaughter the enemies of God at an alarming rate. Why? On his deathbed, Joshua explains that allowing these Baal-worshippers to survive will only ruin everything he and Moses had fought so hard to acquire.

Sure enough, the Hebrews failed to wipe out the Canaanites, and throughout the books of Judges, Kings, and Chronicles, the Hebrews struggle with worshipping these Canaanite gods like a junkie unable to conquer addiction.

So why was Rahab spared?

First of all, look at her response to the two spies who she hid and protected:

[Joshua 2:11] And as soon as we had heard these things, our hearts did melt, neither did there remain any more courage in any man, because of you: for the LORD your God, he is God in heaven above, and in earth beneath.

Certainly, she was afraid and might have seen this as a "Get-out-of-Jail Free" card. But if you look at the second half of her answer, she readily acknowledged God. Did she do this just to save her neck or did she really repent?

Ironically, the mercy of the two spies is not celebrated. A thousand years later, the author of Hebrews even brings her up between the examples of Moses and the Judges:

[Hebrews 11:31] By faith the harlot Rahab perished not with them that believed not, when she had received the spies with peace.

So it was indeed her faith that saved her, and because of this faith, she helped the spies escape Jericho by lowering them down by a rope (or cord) through a window.

Jiving the Genealogy

What does any of this have to do with Christmas?

Perhaps it is best for you to just skip ahead to chapter three, where Matthew, Mark, and Luke will introduce you to Mary and Joseph. But starting there is leaving out so much backstory, including the story of Rahab and her rope. But even Matthew and Luke decided to include long genealogies of Jesus when introducing the story. In those two lists, there is a sea of names that hold little meaning to most people. At first glance, the basic point of the two lists are to essentially show how Jesus descended from King David (through two lines even) as well as descending from good Hebrew stock through Abraham (and even all the way back to Adam).

That's nice.

Quite impressive, actually.

Both Matthew and Luke felt including a genealogy was important, but if you look at the two lists, they appear to be quite a mess. While Luke starts in the present and goes back through the generations, Matthew began in the past with Abraham and worked his way through the generations to Jesus. Luke uses the phrase "the son of" while Matthew uses the word "begat." Abraham, King David, Joseph. The point of showing his lineage as some sort of "proof" quickly falls apart when you hold the two lists side-by-side.

Let's talk about that for a minute.

Who is Jesus's paternal grandfather?

Okay, I concede you could shout out that Joseph was not his biological father and that the list, because of this point, is really worthless. But imagine sitting around Nazareth with a young Jesus, and Joseph says to Jesus, "Hey Jesus, go get *my* father. Go get grandpa."

According to <u>Matthew 1:16,</u> Jesus should look for Grandpa Jacob; however, if you look at <u>Luke 3:23</u>, Jesus would go get Grandpa Heli. For both Matthew and Luke, this would not have been ancient historical records. Joseph's father would have been *known* by people still alive. So what gives?

I've heard all sorts of interpretations of the two genealogies, and before I get sucked into these whirlpools, I'll admit that there are all sorts of ways to take this section. Perhaps Heli is just a nickname for Jacob? Or…perhaps it is another example of countless other Biblical figures who have been double-named (Jacob/Israel, Saul/Paul, Joseph/Barnabas). I've heard theories that one list is for Joseph and the other list is for Mary. Hmm? Mary and Joseph might have both belonged to the same tribe, so this is possible. Considering Jesus and Joseph are not "biological-ly" related, I can see the importance of showing Mary's line instead of Joseph's.

But the number of names is grossly different, seeming to in-sinuate many extra generations in Luke's account. Another problem is that the lists will weave back together with similar names only to fly apart again.

(Rahab…you were making a point about Rahab)

Early Christians noticed the apparent differences between Matthew and Luke, and an early church historian named Euse-bius quoted an older historian by the name of Africanus who had a very long explanation that I'll quickly sum up so I can get back to Rahab. Africanus explained that there was a difference between the legal line and the biological line. Grandpa Jacob "begat" Joseph biologically, but legally, Joseph's father was Heli. Complicated, huh?

In this regard, it makes sense why the educated physician Luke would have chosen to research and include the "legal" line of Christ, which includes many more names than the biological line of Matthew. With Luke including the legal "son of" list, it is not surprising to find some different names, but in Matthew's biological list, there are four women included in that list, includ-ing (you guessed it)…Rahab.

Along with Rahab, the other three women mentioned have no good reason to be included. After all, three of them would be considered sexually immoral women, so why would Matthew make a point to include these three women in a genealogy meant to help prove the divinity of Jesus Christ. No wholesome Hebrew or Jewish women were even mentioned. Why bother bringing shame to the list? Also, in a list that meant to prove Jesus as the "King of the Jews," Matthew included two who were considered to be foreigners (and you know the Hebrew marriage policy regarding that).

Bringing up Bathsheba

First, let's look at the wife of Uriah, Bathsheba. Interestingly, Matthew does not include her name. Instead, he writes that King David "begat Solomon of her that had been the wife of Uriah." Ouch. The Luke lineage focuses on Nathan, the legal son of King David. David's seduction of Bathsheba is told in 2 Samuel 11. David's actions resulted in the murder of Uriah and the eventual demise of his own kingdom after a civil war.

But out of this relationship came Solomon, the biological ancestor of "One greater than Solomon," Jesus of Nazareth.

Regarding Ruth

Next, let's learn about a woman who came a few generations prior to Bathsheba, Ruth. Of the four names on this list, Ruth is probably the most famous. After all, she has her own book of the Bible in which...wait, what happens in Ruth?

The book of Ruth is a story of loyalty and friendship, in which Ruth stays by the side of her mother-in-law through all sorts of hardships. According to Mosaic Law (Deut 25:7-9), when your brother dies, you have an obligation to marry his childless widow (remember Heli and Jacob?). Ruth's husband died, leaving her without a child. Later in the story, another Hebrew man, Boaz, fell in love with Ruth; however, according to Mosaic Law, another of her former husband's relatives had a better claim. In the end, true love triumphed and Boaz and Ruth got married, allowing Ruth to become the great-grandmother of King David. So, the two strangest things about this story is how Mosaic law was set-aside *and* how a Moabite woman was able to marry into the genealogy.

Just like the Canaanites, the Moabites were considered to be enemies of the Hebrew people. To the Hebrews, the Moabites were redneck, inbred (seriously, read about Lot), hillbillies (yes, they lived in the mountains), who frequently caused problems through the generations. Again, Matthew's decision to emphasize Ruth is beginning to form some sort of point, isn't it?

The Truth about Tamar

Before Ruth and Bathsheba, there was a woman named Tamar. If you are not familiar with Tamar, you probably just had a bashful Sunday school teacher. Genesis 38 is a bit…awkward.

One of the reasons Tamar is not well known is that it is sandwiched by the story of Joseph. Despite Joseph being the most "beloved" of the twelve sons of Jacob, we know Jesus is descended from the line of Judah, the fourth born son. Previously, we already saw how being the firstborn son (Esau) does not mean you inherit everything of value (Jacob being part of the Christ bloodline). Yet Genesis 38 has a very strange twist.

To begin with, Judah had some impulse problems that resulted in him marrying a Canaanite woman named Shuah (this is before Rahab and Joshua) who gave him three sons: Er, Onan, and Shelah. Jacob then arranged a marriage between Er and Tamar (from the list); however, Er ended up dying without giving Tamar any children (see <u>Deut. 25</u> again). To make things right, Judah gave Tamar to his other son Onan so that they might give dead Er a legal son (the Luke genealogy) despite the fact that he was dead.

Strange, huh?

It gets stranger.

Onan didn't want to give his dead brother an heir by impregnating poor Tamar, so Onan did something most Sunday school teachers **really** don't want to discuss. Onan's defiance resulted in a very short life, leaving Tamar as a widow (again).

According to the Deuteronomy law, Tamar was still owed a husband but Judah's third son, Shelah was still a boy. So Judah sent her away until he grew up.

A few years pass.

Having forgotten his pledge to Tamar, Judah happens to be near Tamar's home, and when she hears Shelah is of age, she dresses up like a widow and sits on a corner. After working in the fields, Judah sees a woman sitting beside the road and assumes she was a prostitute (big mistake). Tamar keeps her true identity hidden, allows Judah to take advantage of her, and get impregnated by her father-in-law.

Ready for the hypocrisy?

When Judah learns that Tamar is pregnant (instead of saving herself for Shelah), he decides to burn her for being a harlot.

Luckily, she had proof of the father's identity, who turned out to be...Judah!

So Judah spares her, and thus Matthew lists the two sons, Phares and Zara, to be listed as Judah's son, bypassing poor Shelah. During the birth of the twins, a strange phenomenon happens with one of the boys emerging breach. The nurse quickly puts a scarlet cord around the child's hand to determine who was born first (like that really mattered).

It is this scarlet thread that really caught my attention. Scarlet is the color of blood. A thread is also a line. Blood line?

Tying it All Together

Look again at the story of Rahab. Remember how she saved the spies, who then spared her life? After helping them escape from a rope, they promised to spare her if she...tied a scarlet line in her window (Joshua 2:21). What are the odds of the phrase "scarlet line" and "scarlet thread" both being used with matriarchs in the bloodline of Christ?

Neither woman should have naturally been part of the genealogy of Jesus. Rahab was the enemy, for crying out loud! Tamar should have been Shelah's wife (or Onan's...or Er's) yet the bloodline weaves its way through these two women.

And this also makes sense for the other two women in the list. Both Bathsheba and Ruth were widowers involved in scandals.

So why did Matthew insist on naming these four women in a list that is trying to establish Jesus' divine right as the King of the Jews?

The Scarlet Thread shows that we (murderers, foreigners, liars, fourth-born sons, adulterers) all had a part in the story. The genealogy of Christ wasn't neat and simple, was it? It also shows that salvation wasn't just for the Jews. Moabite and Canaanite women were featured prominently to show that the Christ was more than just a Messiah for the descendants of Abraham.

And the metaphor of a Scarlet Thread illustrates how this bloodline not only connects to the past but also our future. As I argued earlier, I am not even sure if Matthew's list makes biological sense. It is Joseph's list, right? So maybe this bloodline is not about Christ but about us. We are the Scarlet Thread.

Matthew 27:28 describes how a scarlet robe was put upon Christ at the Crucifixion, along with the crown of thorns. Christ literally carried our sins (the Scarlet Threads) to the cross.

How does Christ return?

Revelation 19:13 describes how Christ will ride in on a white horse, with eyes blazing like fire, and royal crowns upon his head. But what is he wearing? He is wearing a robe that is the color of blood (scarlet). If this metaphor works, he is wearing humanity upon his shoulders as a conquering champion.

Which is what the Jews were expecting in the 1st Century.

But as we learned with Tamar, Rahab, Ruth, and Bathsheba, even the concept of the Christ did not go according to man's definition.

CHAPTER TWO

WHAT TO EXPECT... WHEN YOU'RE EXPECTING THE CHRIST

Jesus Christ did not have a father named Joseph Christ. Christ is not a last name. While some Christians might think Jesus Christ is a full, proper name, the word Christ is actually a title. The word translation gets a little messy, but essentially, Christ means "the Anointed One," or the Messiah.

So Jesus Christ really needs an article to become Jesus the Christ. After the crucifixion and resurrection, Jesus is referred to as Jesus Christ (or Christ Jesus) much more often. Even after two thousand years, explaining the purpose of the Christ is quite complicated at times, so it is really hard to imagine what the innkeeper, the shepherds, or even the Magi would have expected from the Christ.

If you want to jump right into the Christmas story, you still might want to jump right to chapter nine (but you'd be missing a lot of really nerdy stuff).

Seeking the Christ

The Christ did not come out of the blue. People in the first century expected a Christ, even if they didn't quite know what to expect. Want an example? Read a little of John 4. In this chapter, you will read about a Samaritan woman who meets Jesus at a well. In case you don't know, Samaritans were not respected by the Jews, and this woman probably held even less respect. Yet after having a fairly deep philosophic conversation about salvation, the woman says to Jesus:

[John 4:25] I know that Messiah cometh, which is called Christ. When He is come, He will tell us all things.

This Samaritan woman is trashy, probably uneducated, possibly a pagan (see mountain worship references) and definitely born on the wrong side of the tracks, but even SHE knew a Messiah, or Christ, was coming to set things straight.

She expected it.

Another example of expecting the Christ can be seen with Simon the Rock (sounds like a wrestler, I'll stick with just Peter). In Mark 8:29, Jesus asks Peter who He is. Peter answers with **"Thou art the Christ."** Peter had several swing-and-a-miss moments, but this time he hit a homerun. But Peter had a good idea that Jesus was the Christ *long* before this public confession. If you look at John 1:42, you will see how Peter had already been looking for the Christ.

His brother Andrew was a disciple of John the Baptist when Jesus showed up to be baptized. When that scene concludes, Andrew goes running off to find his brother Simon (Peter), saying, **"we have found the Messiah (which is translated as Christ)."**

There are all sorts of ways to interpret Andrew's meaning. Remember, this is thirty years after a dozen or more figures all witnessed the birth of the Christ—only to have Jesus disappear. Joseph and Mary took Jesus to Egypt, remember? It is possibly that by the time they returned to Nazareth, they could hide his divine identity from the neighbors. There were no miracles until *after* the baptism. How frustrating would it be to be the Magi, Shepherds, Anna, Simeon, or even Herod—and know Jesus is out there somewhere but not know which infant, child, young adult, or thirty-year-old man it really was?

Another possibility is that John the Baptist talked about the coming Christ. With this possibility, Andrew certainly would have written home to his family that his mentor openly predicted the coming of the Christ, just as Elijah promised to return before the coming of the Christ. Peter undoubtedly told his brother something to this effect: Hey, if the Christ does show up, come and get me!

OR...Peter and Andrew were two devout Jews who simply knew their scriptures, and in the harsh environment of Roman rule, they simply prayed for a deliverer. Upon hearing the voice of God, and the Holy Spirit descending like a dove, Andrew knew the Christ had come.

Peter expected it.

But what exactly did they expect?

In hindsight, it is easy to roll your eyes at the disciples and followers for not quite getting what was happening in front of them. Again and again, we see foot-in-mouth moments (often Peter) that show how they struggled with the concept of the Christ. Even two thousand years later, Christianity is divided into a hundred factions that have varying interpretations of how to view the Christ or what his complex purpose had been.

Buried in the Old Testament are dozens of Christ prophecies that seem like it should have been painfully obvious to any Pharisee or Sadducee that Jesus was the Christ. Many Christians struggle with the idea that modern Jews can't recognize all the signs in their own texts. But even John, who trained with both the Baptist and the Christ, didn't catch all the details. Do you remember John at the open tomb? **"For as yet they knew not the scripture, that He must rise again from the dead."** Remember, it was on the Road to Emmaus that an undercover Jesus had to reveal the meaning of the scriptures:

> **[Luke 24:45] Then he opened their understanding, that they might understand the scriptures.**

So if someone living in the time and very presence of Jesus misses a few details, who are we to judge?

But in the beginning of Genesis, all the way through the Book of Malachi, the cumulative details about the Christ created a collection of dots, that when connected, create a pretty clear representation of the Christ. So let's review.

Clue #1: "The Seed of a Woman."

In Genesis 3:15, we see one of the earliest references to the Christ with this "punishment/prophecy." Remember that Satan, Adam, and Eve are all getting punished here, but hidden in Eve's punishment is that Eve's offspring will bring damage to Satan (bruised head) and that Satan will in return bring damage to her offspring (bruised heel). If you were an angry Satan, now you are even more upset. But for Adam and Eve, this is their darkest hour to date, in which they will be cast out of the garden and out of the presence of God, all because of Satan. After the depression of their fallen state wore off, they undoubtedly would see a little hope (and revenge) in this veiled prophecy. This clue is confirmed with Galatians 4:4.

Clue #2: "A Descendant of Abra(ha)m."

For generations, the cast of candidates exploded, then greatly narrowed (Noah's Ark), and then quickly began to bloom again. Around the time of Nimrod, the Tower of Babel, and the Division of Peleg, God looked out at all of his "candidates" and chose Abram. While Genesis 12:3 isn't super specific about Jesus or the Christ, it effectively picks Abraham as the Bloodline, putting the two sons of Abraham, (Ishmael and Isaac) on Satan's "Most Wanted and Most Persecuted" list. Matthew 1:1 confirms this clue.

Clue #3: "A Descendant of Isaac."

We learned from the Scarlet Thread that the first-born son concept is not one that God follows exclusively. Genesis 17:19

clarifies that while Ishmael's descendants will be many, it will be Isaac through which the covenant will flow. So the Hebrews began God's chosen people.

With this "pat on the head" proclamation, Satan unleashes his full arsenal on the Hebrews just like we saw when God praised Job. The chosen people are subsequently tempted and tormented, with many turning to evil. Yet the promise had been made, and as Luke noted in 3:34, it was through this line that we were given Jesus.

Clue #4: "A Descendant of Jacob."

Once again, the Scarlet Thread does not weave its way through to the first-born son. Isaac had two sons, Esau and Jacob, but only one was to receive the covenant. Genesis 25:29 begins the story of how Jacob kinda steals his birthright away from his older twin brother Esau, who despised it. But it is actually a foreign sorcerer who really makes this switch to Jacob more obvious. In Numbers 24:17, Balaam the sorcerer lets all the bad guys know that they are powerless from stopping God's plans. Balaam says:

> **[Numbers 24:17] I shall see him, but not now: I shall behold him, but not nigh: there shall come a Star out of Jacob, and a Sceptre shall rise out of Israel, and shall smite the corners of Moab, and destroy all the children of Sheth.**

While this prophecy certainly had short time implications, it also hearkens to the second coming of Christ. Matthew 1:2 and 2:2 also confirms Jesus as a descendant of Jacob as well as connecting to the star of the Magi.

Clue #5: "The Tribe of Judah."

For many modern Christians, the word Hebrew is synony-mous with the word Jew, especially if you are bored with the books of Kings or Chronicles. The cast of candidates grew vast again after Jacob had twelve sons. Would the Christ come through his first-born son, Reuben? Nope. How about Jacob's two favorites, Joseph and Benjamin? Nope and double nope. Then obviously it will be through his priestly line, the Levites? Not quite. It is through Judah, his fourth born, that the Christ shall come:

> **[Genesis 49:8] Judah, thou art he whom they brethren shall praise: thy hand shall be in the neck of thine enemies; thy father's children shall bow down before thee. Judah is a lion's whelp: from the prey, my son, thou art gone up: he stooped down, he crouched as a lion, and as an old lion; who shall rouse him up? The scepter shall not depart from Judah, nor a lawgiver from between his feet, until Shiloh come, and unto him shall the gathering of the people be.**

Again, as a short-term prophecy, the two southern tribes sur-vived all sorts of conquest and genocide from their enemies. But as a long term prophecy, you can see hints at the Battle of Ar-mageddon, the Valley of Dry Bones, the Millennial Kingdom, and Judgment Day in this final prophecy from Jacob. The scep-ter is again mentioned, which really begins to shape the Christ as a king and lawgiver.

Clue #6: "Heir to the Throne of David."

Now by the era of Mary and Joseph, the throne had been vacant for hundreds of years since Nebuchadnezzar destroyed the kingdom. While the Hasmoneans brought back Jewish leadership, Israel was ruled by a foreigner by the name of Herod, leaving the people to wonder who "legally" is the blood heir of David. Isaiah 9:6-7 certainly gave these leaderless people some hope that a child would be born to restore "David's Throne" and deliver an eternal kingdom.

The problem is that King David had a lot of legitimate and illegitimate heirs—nineteen are named in the Bible. So good luck tracking them down nearly six centuries later. You can see why Matthew and Luke would have been confused as to which list to use when both seemed to connect the Scarlet Thread to Jesus.

Clue #7: "Born in Bethlehem."

Okay, now we're talking. That is at least a little more specific, which is why Herod (and probably Satan) had it on the radar. We know Clue #7 was commonly known because Herod's guys expected this as a certainty. When the Magi showed up in Jerusalem, Herod probably thought "Are you sure you don't want to check Bethlehem?" Herod expected the Magi to do his dirty work of specifically identifying WHICH baby was the Christ (thank goodness for a little angelic detour). His reason for doing this was a few passages from Micah 5:2:

[Micah 5:2] But thou, Bethlehem Ephratah, though thou be little among the thousands of Judah, yet out of thee shall he

come forth until me that is to be ruler in Israel; whose going forth have been from old, from everlasting.

Micah goes on to talk about how the Christ shall be both a shepherd as well as a warrior who shall witness the gathering of the remnant. It is no wonder Herod was frightened by the idea of the Christ.

Clue #8: "Born of a Virgin."

Scoffers love to mock the virgin birth as a scientific impossibility, and this chapter is not going to get into the science of Mary. But Luke, who was a physician, probably had a good understanding of basic reproductive science. It is the doctor, not a shepherd or fisherman, who laid it on the line with the virgin birth.

Why?

The concept of a god made flesh is a bit surreal unto itself and hearkens back to the Greek myths of maidens being impregnated by Zeus. Yet Luke the researcher must have dug up the truth after talking to Mary or others and insisted in sharing this story in his Gospel. After all, it does fulfill Isaiah 7:14:

[Isaiah 7:14] Therefore the Lord himself shall give you a sign; Behold, a virgin shall conceive, and bear a son, and shall call his name Immanuel (God is with us). Butter and honey shall he eat, that he may know to refuse evil, and choose the good.

Of the twenty translations I read of this verse, nineteen wrote virgin. The version that used "young woman" was the Tanakh, the Hebrew Bible used by modern Jews. Even if you were to go with this "watered down" version (after all, what is miraculous about a young woman *giving birth?*), the prophecy still let them know that the Christ would be born rather than descending on a beam of light.

It even added a little detail that the Christ will have the classic "Tree of Knowledge" test, involving Good and Evil. This verse insinuates there would be more at stake even after the birth.

Clue #9: "Slaughter of the Infants."

Jeremiah 31 also mentioned a virgin as well as others who will be filled with joy, but the tone dramatically changes by verse 15:

[Jeremiah 31:15 Thus saith the LORD; 'A voice was heard in Ramah, Lamentation and bitter weeping. Rachel weeping for her children; Refused to be comforted for her children, Because they were not.'

The Rachel being talked about is the beloved wife of Jacob. Her tomb is currently a tourist stop in—Bethlehem. So any Pharisee that dug up the prophecy about being born in Bethlehem also knew the coming of the Christ would be bittersweet.

Clue #10: "Growing Up."

There are certainly many more clues about the Christ than just ten, but many of the others deal with his life and death—not his birth and origins. King Herod and all his men were pretty certain about the Bethlehem birth, yet in hindsight, we know that Jesus wasn't really *from* Bethlehem. Mary and Joseph both seem to be from Nazareth, go to Bethlehem for the birth, and then...? <u>Hosea 11:1</u> seems to come out of left field to answer that question. It says:

[Hosea 11:1] When Israel was a child, then I loved him, and called my son out of Egypt.

What happened? Mary and Joseph fled Herod's wrath and stayed in Egypt. After Herod's death, Jesus was called out of Egypt. There is another obscure prophecy that Matthew mentions. In <u>Matthew 2:23</u>, he writes about the exile in Egypt:

[Matthew 2:23] And he (Joseph) came and dwelt in a city called Nazareth, that it might be fulfilled which was spoken by the prophets, 'He shall be called a Nazarene.'

But what the heck is Matthew talking about? For centuries, scholars have been clueless about the source of Matthew's prophecy, and without knowing the source, have twisted this verse in a variety of directions. Regardless, Matthew had a popular saying (lost to us now) that the Christ would be called a Nazarene. Matthew's assumption was that this had something to do with Nazareth.

So by looking at those "top ten" clues, you can begin to understand what a first century believer might have expected, but this is just the tip of the iceberg. The Book of Psalms, for example, has dozens of little references. By themselves, none of them are super-obvious, but when you put them all together in a list (which is what I'll do on the next page) it is pretty impressive. While some of the previously mentioned prophecies were known and mentioned, these 'buried" prophecies were probably only understood ***after*** the Holy Spirit came and enlightened the believers.

More Clues about the Christ

I'm going to give you the verse and a very simplistic para-phrase of each verse:

Psalm 2:7	**The Christ will be the Son of God.**
Psalm 8:2	**The Christ will be praised by Children.**
Psalm 8:6	**The Christ will be the Ruler of All.**
Psalm 16:10	**The Christ will rise from the dead.**
Psalm 16:10	**The Christ is the only way to avoid Sheol.**
Psalm 22:1	**The Christ will be crucified.**
Psalm 22:7	**The Christ will be derided.**
Psalm 22:16	**The Christ will have hands and feet pierced.**
Psalm 22:18	**The Christ's clothes will be divided.**
Psalm 34:20	**The Christ's bones will be unbroken.**
Psalm 35:11	**The Christ will be unfairly tried, convicted.**
Psalm 35:19	**The Christ will be hated without cause.**
Psalm 40:7	**The Christ will delight in God's will.**
Psalm 41:9	**The Christ will be betrayed by a friend.**
Psalm 68:18	**The Christ will ascend to Heaven.**
Psalm 69:9	**The Christ will have zeal.**
Psalm 69:21	**The Christ will be given vinegar and gall.**
Psalm 109:4	**The Christ will pray for his enemies.**
Psalm 109:8	**The Christ's betrayer will be replaced.**
Psalm 110:1	**The Christ will rule over enemies.**
Psalm 110:4	**The Christ will be a priest forever.**
Psalm 118:22	**The Christ will be a chief stone.**
Psalm 118:26	**The Christ will come in the name of the LORD.**

Wow! What a list, huh?

So if you were a Pharisee or shepherd, with a keen interest in the Christ, there were all sorts of prophecies to sort through.

For us, we can specifically see which of these happened during his time on earth and which are still going to happen during his 2nd Coming, but for first generation followers, it is no wonder they expected Jesus to defeat the Romans and take the throne of David for himself. It would have been very difficult to reconcile Psalm 110:4 with Psalm 22:16.

There is also a thought amongst theologians that the Christ made all sorts of cameo appearances during the Old Testament. Who visited Moses in his tent? In other words, you have two choices. The Christ stayed in a special place during the Old Testament era or he was a spiritual being capable of visiting earth.

It does explain what the prophets would see when they claimed to see God. Because of this, the ANGEL OF THE LORD references are often viewed as Christ appearances.

Perhaps one of the strangest Christ predictions can be found in the Book of Malachi, which is the last book of the Old Testament. One of the reasons why this book was placed at the end was because of its *very* specific prediction about the coming of the Christ. Two thousand years after the birth of the Christ, we have a better understanding of the two phases of the Christ, with the second phrase happening in the Book of Revelation, but to a first century believer, Malachi sounded a little End Times-y.

In a nutshell, this prophecy says that **before** the Christ arrives, God will send Elijah back to the Hebrews to prepare the way. In preparing the way, Malachi chapter 3 & 4 drops phrases like "refiners fire" and "purify" along with **"turn their hearts"** lest **"I come and strike the earth."**

So Elijah was supposed to make sure the Boss doesn't get angry and throw a fit when he arrives. Many people now believe these verses in Malachi are End Times predictions, and as a result, they often feel Elijah is *obviously* going to be one of the Two Witnesses described in The Book of Revelation.

Possibly.

Remember the last time we saw Elijah? That's right, he was going off to Heaven on a fiery chariot. Hard to forget that. Jesus's disciples certainly didn't forget this vivid description, and once they realized Jesus was the Christ, they were really confused by the Malachi prophecy. In <u>Matthew 17:10</u>, one of the disciples asks,

[Matthew 17:10] Why then say scribes say Elias (Elijah) must first come?

For now, I'm going to leave the question unanswered (until Chapter 7), but it is a cool reminder how the disciples had clear and obvious expectations of the Christ prior to his arrival.

The Backstory of the Christ

Now this last section is going to get a little weird.

Because Revelation 12 *is* a little weird.

For two thousand years, the entire book of Revelation has been giving Christians fits (and 1st century Jews all shout out…HA!). Just like we had prophecies of the coming Christ, the Book of Revelation is a preview of the End Times. We get angels, Antichrists, and all sorts of wild imagery to sort through. Some see the whole book as hyperbolic metaphors of events that happened in the 1st Century and others see it as literal clues that will happen during the final seven years of our world. I've read dozens upon dozens of interpretations of these poetic chapters and verses, and one of the most nebulous sections is that darn chapter 12.

So go ahead and reference your Bible now.

To paraphrase, we see a woman who gives birth. Then we see a dragon try to kill her and her baby. Then we see a war break out between good angels and bad angels. Then there is a loud speech. Then more running and chasing. Then the dragon develops some digestive issues. Finally, it ends with the equivalent of the dragon saying, "I'll be back."

Cue chapter 13.

Huh?

Even the simplified paraphrase is confusing, isn't it? This chapter bothered me for a long time because it had so many possibilities, especially the beginning and the ending sections. But let's look at the context of what was happening to John and the Book of Revelation before we start splitting this prophecy apart.

So far, John was sitting on the island of Patmos when he gets a bunch of messages for the seven churches (Ch 1-3). In chapters 4 & 5, he sees a vision of Heaven in which Jesus proves himself to be worthy and is given a scroll to open.

Beginning with chapter 6, Jesus begins to open each seal one at a time and all sorts of weird and wild stuff happens to humanity. Once the scroll is fully opened, it seems as if we are in the last days of the End Times. Chapter 8 begins the Seven Trumpets section that seems to be reminiscent of the Ten Plagues of

Egypt. After these Seven Trumpets (and before the Seven Bowls of Wrath), we get Chapter 12.

Why?

So far, all of these prophecies were about humanity. The last section of Revelation is about Satan, the Antichrist and Company, Death and Hades, and the armies of evil. Epic stuff. Why show Satan and the gang getting punished? If you are a human, who cares? Well, the Evil Ones have a back-story, don't they? I believe Revelation 12 is a fuller explanation than we get in Genesis (which was totally Adam and Eve's POV). In order to understand the punishment, we need to first understand the crime.

Revelation 12 is not prophecy—it is a flashback.

While the whole prophecy is a bit messy to decipher, there is one section that seems clear to me.

[Revelation 12:9] And the great dragon was cast out, that old serpent, called the Devil, and Satan, which deceiveth the whole world: he was cast to the earth, and his angels were cast out with him.

This is verse 9 of 17. It is right in the middle of this prophecy about the woman, birth, war, speech, and revenge.

Now take a look at something Jesus said during his time on earth. Luke 10:18 is the end of the story about how Jesus sent out his gang of disciples, and how they were blown away by the authority they had over agents of evil like demons. Now, I'm not sure if Jesus would roll his eyes when they said **"Lord, even the demons are subject to us in Your name,"** but he does sound a little snarky with his response:

[Luke 10:18] And He said to them, 'I beheld Satan fall as lightning from heaven. Behold, I give unto you power to tread on serpents and scorpions and over all the power of the enemy, and nothing shall be by any means hurt you. Notwithstanding in this rejoice not, that the spirits are subject to you; but rather rejoice, because your names are written in heaven.'

The kernel of information in this passage is Jesus referencing that He was there when Satan fell from heaven. Past tense. Flashback. Another interesting reference from Jesus can be found in:

[John 8:44] You are of your father the devil, and the lusts of your father ye will do. He was a murderer from the beginning, and abode not in truth, because there is no truth in him.

Murderer from the beginning? Having read Genesis, I do not remember any mention or reference to "murder" in the Tree of Knowledge scene. What is Jesus talking about? Well, there is another cryptic reference given by Jesus in:

[Matthew 11:12] And from the days of John the Baptist until now, the kingdom of heaven suffereth violence, and the violent take it by force.

Now, as with most prophecies, there can be dual meanings, so I do not entirely limit Chapter 12 to *only* flashback. But let's just explore it as a flashback and explanation of what happened around the time Adam and Eve were walking out of the garden. Before we can do that, let's talk about the origins of Jesus for a moment.

The verses we just discussed show Jesus referencing the fact that he has been around since the beginning, right? "I was there when…" The Book of John opens with a very poetic explanation that Jesus=Word=God=beginning by saying:

[John 1:1] In the beginning was the Word, and the Word was with God, and the Word was God. He was in the beginning with God. All things were made through Him, and without Him nothing was made that was made. In Him was life, and the life was the light of men. And the light shines in the darkness, and the darkness did not comprehend it.

The early church grappled with this concept until they hammered out the Nicene Creed. They struggled with the idea of Jesus, God, and the Holy Spirit as separate entities. It's almost more than a human can reckon, huh? I think John did a nice job explaining it in the above paragraph, even though I'm not quite sure what that means. Genesis uses the plural word "Elohim" along with a reference in 3:22 that says:

[Genesis 3:2] And the LORD God said, 'Behold, the man is become as one of us…'

Us=plural. Yet the Early Christians struggled with the finer details of the Trinity.

It doesn't matter one iota.

Actually, it did. This phrase actually comes from the Council of Nicaea. As they hammered out the Nicene Creed, they debated the wording of it. Some felt that Jesus was "of similar substance" while others believed Jesus was "of the same substance" as God. The Greek spelling of these two phrases were only different because of the letter iota.

In the end, the Council of Nicaea determined Jesus was "of the same substance" as God, leaving most of Christendom to scratch their heads and shrug.

Imagine a really big ball of clay (five gallon bucket size). The ball of clay is the Trinity.

In the Beginning…Elohim.

The ball of clay is God, Jesus, and the Holy Spirit. In the beginning was the Word? The Word was with God. The Word was God. So now, along with the ball of clay, we create…the Universe. Picture a coffee cup (yes, I am writing this at 7:59 on a Sunday Morning). Despite being really big, the Universe is still smaller than our big ball of clay. In fact, picture that big five-gallon ball of clay wrapping itself entirely around that coffee cup.

Let there be light…

A lot of people imagine Day One of creation from our human POV. We picture a sunrise, right? Or a solar system view of the sun peering around the moon to illuminate a blue globe, right? Hold on a second! What happened on Day Four?

[Genesis 1:14] And God said, Let there be lights in the firmament of the heaven to divide the day from the night; and let them be for signs, and for seasons, and for days, and years: 15And let them be for lights in the firmament of the heaven to give light upon the earth: and it was so. 16And God made two great lights; the greater light to rule the day, and the lesser light to rule the night: [he made] the stars also. 17And God set them in the firmament of the heaven to give light upon the earth, 18And to rule over the day and over the night, and to divide the light from the darkness: and God saw that [it was] good. 19And the evening and the morning were the fourth day.

Umm…let there be light (again?)…

So on Day Four, God created the sun, moon, and stars. THIS light is what gave us seasons. THIS light is what lets us see stuff in the dark. THIS light helps us tell time. So what happened on Day One?

[Genesis 1:3] And God said, Let there be light: and there was light. 4 And God saw the light, that [it was] good: and God divided the light from the darkness. 5 And God called the light Day, and the darkness he called Night. And the evening and the morning were the first day.

But if it wasn't the sun…

Characteristics of the Holy Spirit

Let's go back to the big five-gallon ball of clay.

Elohim (the big ball of clay) creates the empty universe (the coffee cup). But Elohim existed before the coffee cup. Elohim cannot fit inside of the coffee cup. Elohim exists outside of the coffee cup. Elohim surrounds the coffee cup. Yet Elohim also wants to fill the coffee cup (which is filled with darkness).

Let there be light…

Let there be Light.

Picture the Holy Spirit for a moment.

Pentecost. Tongues of Fire.

The Baptism of Jesus.

Descending *like* a dove.

The Holy Spirit is very abstract. It fills us. It is part of Elohim, and thus, has existed since the beginning along with God and Jesus. It comes. It goes. It fills. It surrounds.

It exists inside of our Universe?

Duh!

Ah…Let there be Light!

Picture the big ball of clay and the coffee cup. Could it be that on Day One, God's substance enters into the universe in tangible "form"? The creative force, the hand of God, slips into the space of the coffee cup, bringing Light. Is the clay inside of the coffee cup different than the clay outside of the coffee cup?

Nope.

Does it have a different purpose than the clay outside of the coffee cup? Uh, I think so?

Without the Holy Spirit, the coffee cup is filled with darkness. It is black coffee with no creamer (okay, I'll stop with the analogies). The coffee cup is not the clay. It is Darkness. By putting Light=Holy Spirit=His substance into the coffee cup, the appearance of God has changed even though it is the same exact clay. It is the clay the Universe can see.

What about the clay outside of the Universe?

John says something very profound a few verses after explaining the Word (Jesus) and God. He says in verse 18:

[John 1:18] No man hath seen God at any time.

What about Moses on Mount Horeb? According to John, NO ONE. If God exists outside of his creation, how can anyone IN his creation see outside of creation?

Oh…

So what did all of those people in the Old Testament, who existed only inside the coffee cup of our universe, actually see when they claimed to see God? What gave Moses a sunburn? What did Jacob see in that wrestling match?

On Day One, I believe the Hand of God made an appearance in the coffee cup of our universe. God is Good. God is Light. The Light that illuminated our universe was not physical light (that came on Day Four); it was Spiritual Light. What do we call this aspect of God? The Holy Spirit.

Is the Holy Spirit any different than God?

Yes!

Yes?

No?

No!

John did his best to explain it using algebra: Word=Jesus=Light=God=Word.

Keep reading those opening verses. It goes round and round and round. Contrasted against all of this is the Darkness. Remember how Jesus referenced being around at the beginning? Jesus was there with God, wasn't he? In the same way, the Holy Spirit is the same substance as God. The Holy Spirit is the same clay as God.

Does your coffee cup have an opening?

Sure does, right?

Our five-gallons of clay totally surrounds the coffee cup, and it entered into the coffee cup through the opening (Heaven?). Through this window of Heaven, God's creative hand forms everything on Day Two, Day Three, Day Four (okay, now we have a sun), Day Five, Day Six (hey look, Adam).

At this point, Adam sees God. But what does he see exactly? Can Adam see the clay outside of the coffee cup? Nope. Can he see his creator? Yep, in fact, he walks with Elohim. Is Adam walking with the same substance as what exists outside of the coffee cup?

I think so.

For Adam, and all of us since, we have rationalized this different form of God as the Holy Spirit. God=Holy Spirit=Jesus=God. The Trinity is pretty abstract stuff.

Let's get back to the subject of this chapter—the Christ.

A Day in the Garden

(This next part is a flawed analogy to make a point, so bear with me). Picture Adam and Eve in the Garden. There are animals (I picture a platypus swimming in the Gihon River). There are some pretty cool trees. Even Satan is still behaving (hey, Lucifer).

It is Good.

During this walk with God (the Light, the Holy Spirit), do you picture Jesus sitting on a rock?

"Hey God?" Adam asks, "I'm pretty much the most perfect human ever made, so I have a high capacity for abstract thinking and analogies, but WHO IS THAT?"

(At this point, picture the Wizard of Oz). "Oh, Him? Pay no attention to the Man behind the curtain. We'll get to Him later."

Adam is now curious. In fact, he is more curious about the Mystery Man than he is curious about the Tree of Knowledge. "But why is he here? What's his purpose? Is he supposed to be my fishing buddy?"

God is getting impatient. "No, Adam. He is not your fishing buddy. The Christ is here because you and Eve are going to really screw up in the near future, and I made him so that he could be sacrificed so that all of humanity can be saved."

"Oh…"

(faulty analogy over).

My point is that until Adam and Eve actually sinned, there was NO reason to have the Christ show up. Until they sinned, their view of God was probably limited to the walking, talking pillar of light. AFTER the fall, Adam and Eve were given the promise of the Christ.

Yet we are clearly told that the Christ existed since the very beginning of creation as The Word. Yes, he did not become flesh until shortly after Gabriel made the trip to Nazareth, but the Christ existed as the Word since the beginning. Jesus is the same substance as God. In the beginning was the Word.

John explains it for us in:

[1 John 3:8]: He that committeth sin is of the devil; for the devil sinneth from the beginning. For this purpose the Son of God was manifested, that he might destroy the works of the devil.

Jesus was "manifested" to fix a problem.

After Adam and Eve (and Satan) sinned, God promised Eve and Satan that her seed would one day deal with Satan. The prophecy of the Christ began on that day in the Garden of Eden. Adam and Eve fled the garden, but what did Satan do?

(drum roll…) Let's look at Revelation 12.

Again, it is my belief that Revelation 12 is a flashback. It is a full explanation for why the Son of God was manifested. Did Jesus come to die on the cross? Yes. Did Jesus come to sacrifice himself as a Lamb for us? Yes. Did Jesus come to gather up all the righteous people from the Old Testament so they could go to Heaven instead of being stuck in Sheol? Yes. Did Jesus come so that everybody that believes in Him since his crucifixion could also go to Heaven? Yes.

Yet 1 John 3:8 seemed to indicate something else.

It's not just business—it's personal.

Remember how Jesus mentioned Satan was a murderer since the beginning? Remember how Jesus said he saw Satan fall? Remember his reference to war in Heaven? I believe Revelation 12 explains what happened to Satan immediately after the expulsion from the Garden of Eden.

On earth, Adam and Eve are walking off in those fur outfits, crying and sniffling. We'll get back to them later.

But Satan is ticked! Like super ticked.

Granted, he might have been angry prior to this. At some point in time (is there a clock ticking before this?) Satan was consumed by darkness and jealousy about Adam and Eve until the jerk showed up at the tree in the guise of a serpent (I picture a really cool dragon, but each to their own). For Eve to trust him, he obviously belonged in the Garden (see Ezekiel 28:13). Yet tricking Adam and Eve into eating the apple is not the same as attempted murder.

Section A: The Woman.

[Rev 12:1-2] Now a great sign appeared in heaven, a woman clothed with the sun, with the moon under her feet, and on her head a garland of twelve stars. Then being with child, she cried out in labor and in pain to give birth.

Eve?
The Virgin Mary?
Israel?
Christianity?
Again, the beauty of prophecy is that it can mean multiple things. These first two lines have been widely interpreted, but

what if this image is shown to John to represent the Holy Spirit? The Holy Spirit is a man? Let's leave gender out of it for a bit. Let's look at the images we do have. We have light. BIG LIGHT. Epic-sun-and-moon-sized light. Did Eve stand on the sun? Mary? We also have 12. So from the tribes of Israel came Jesus? Perhaps. Or…the reason we have twelve tribes and twelve disciples is to honor or symbolize this "woman" being described here.

When Adam and Eve sinned, all of creation must have groaned. All of creation changed. This "labor" is quite symbolic for what happened to our world. Up in heaven, something else also happened. Christ appeared.

Again, Christ was always there. He was there as part of God's substance before Day One. He probably entered into the Universe on Day One as the creative force that made all things. But on Day Seven, He had not been manifested (even though he was there). Each day after that, he was not seen but was still there. On the day Adam and Eve ate the fruit, the Word spoke. The Christ entered the universe.

Was the Christ born? Jesus was born, but existed prior to taking on flesh. The Christ is the same substance as God. But just as the Holy Spirit was different than God by being in the universe as opposed to the "clay" outside of the universe that was unseen and God, Jesus became even more tangible than the Holy Spirit (who is really big). Jesus is a small piece of clay. Does that mean he is less than God?

NO.

The little piece of clay that is Jesus has always been God and will always be God. But I believe Revelation 12 describes how he and his prophecy entered the universe right after the words were spoken in the Garden.

Section B: The Child.

[Revelation 12:3]: And there appeared another wonder in heaven; and behold a great red dragon, having seven heads and ten horns, and seven crowns upon his heads. [4] And his tail drew the third part of the stars of heaven, and did cast them to the earth: and the dragon stood before the woman which was ready to be delivered, for to devour her child as soon as it was born. [5] And she brought forth a man child, who was to rule all nations with a rod of iron: and her child was caught up unto God, and [to] his throne."

A lot of stuff just happened in those two verses, huh?

Let's start with the Child. It never says explicitly that Jesus=Child in this section, but there are lots of cross-references with the Rod of Iron phrase (Rev 19:15, Rev 2:27, Psalm 2:9, Isaiah 30:14) that give many translators enough confidence to CAPITALIZE the Child as Jesus the Christ. Who else could be taken to the throne of God to hang out until his time comes? Of all the weird concepts in Chapter 12, this is a fairly solid point.

Okay, so if it is the Christ, what exactly is happening here? To paraphrase the whole context, it seems Satan is waiting to kill the Christ as soon as he "makes an appearance." The word birth is a bit perplexing. Jesus was born in Bethlehem, so it almost implies that this is Satan waiting in Bethlehem to eat Jesus. The concept works (Herod) but the narrative falls all apart after this.

Could the Woman be Mary and the Wilderness be Egypt?

Yes, but then the previous section about Mary standing on the sun gets weird. It will also make the following section about THE WAR problematic. In isolation, an argument could be made, but if you back up to the part about the dragon, the context of WHEN this happens is strange.

The dragon's tail throws down a third of the stars of heaven. My assumption is that God, the maker of the universe, understood basic astronomy when this prophecy was given to John. Even with hyperbole, a third of the stars of heaven would be the worst asteroid or meteorological disaster EVER. There were a lot of neutral historians in different continents at the time of Jesus being born in Bethlehem that describes some strange signs but NOTHING close to this. So let's forget about this being astronomical.

I'm going to get into a discussion of angel=star in a later chapter, so right now, we'll just go with a widely viewed assumption that this verse described the Fallen Angels. What caused them to fall? Satan. In Hebrew lore, Satan rallies many of his friends to his cause. Imagine the mindset (if possible) of Satan following the expulsion from the Garden. He tried (successfully) to prove humans were not worthy, yet he ended up getting a prophecy that seemed to threaten his life as well as losing his position. So he complains to his friends about the injustice of it all.

Who is his enemy? Who does he need to be afraid of? As soon as the Word is spoken about the "seed" of Eve being Satan's punisher, it was on. Now, the Christ would not show up for thousands of years in the form of baby Jesus born in a manger (and he tried to kill the baby, too). But for the first time, we had the need of a Christ. If Elohim only existed in two distinct forms

(God beyond his creation and the Holy Spirit within his creation), Satan knew what to watch.

So my crazy theory is that these verses describe how Satan tried to destroy the Christ prophecy by trying to murder the Christ as soon as He became distinct. Remember how Jesus referenced Satan as a murderer? Remember how John wrote "for this purpose" the Christ was "manifested." As Elohim, the Word was there from the beginning, but it was AFTER the fall of Adam, Eve, and Satan that his complex purpose was needed.

So Saint John, John the Evangelist, John the Disciple, James' little brother…the Beloved Disciple…gets a glimpse into the backstory of Jesus and Satan never really seen before. The Book of Revelation is not only the end of the human story but it is also the end of Satan's story. A little later in Revelation (verse 9), it clearly explains that the Red Dragon is Satan. I could write a whole chapter on Dragon/Serpent references, but this is a book about Christmas, so I'll avoid that for today. But Revelation 12 explains what happened back in the day so that we can understand why and what has it in store for the Red Dragon at the end.

Section C: Sanctuary

[Revelation 12:6] And the woman fled into the wilderness, where she hath a place prepared of God, that they should feed her there a thousand two hundred and threescore days.

A few thoughts have gone through my mind on this verse. If the woman is Mary, then this is the trip to Egypt. I also imagine Mount Horeb. I also imagine the place (or the same place) where Jesus went to face the temptations of Satan (he was tend-ed by angels after it was done). I cannot dismiss any of these, but my theory is that the Woman is the Holy Spirit and that all of this is flashback, so I'll explain what I think this is showing under those pretenses.

Before I explain what I think is going on with the Woman (Holy Spirit), I need to get back to the Child (the Christ). Verse 5 talks about how the Christ was taken to God and His throne. Why? Because Satan was planning on murdering the Christ. If Satan was on earth with a third of the Angels (the Garden or Mount Armon) making plans to kill the Christ, Heaven was a safe place to take Him.

I know a lot of people are very fond of <u>Psalm 91</u>, but I like to think Moses wrote it as a love song to his savior. I read it as Moses understanding that the preincarnate Christ has visited him during those 40 years in the wilderness to give him the words (or Words) that will be used by the Word (Jesus) when he comes in the flesh. Remember, Satan quotes this Psalm as if it is some sort of rulebook or guidebook for the Christ. In the wilderness, Jesus rebukes Satan's temptations with the words of Moses. So if this IS a Psalm about the Christ, then:

[Psalm 91] He that dwelleth in the secret place of the most High shall abide under the shadow of the Almighty."

I think Moses understands that the Christ is/was kept in a secret hiding place until he came to earth as Jesus. So if there is a hiding place for Jesus, I think the Woman (Holy Spirit) is also kept safe from Satan.

Again, if Elohim enters into His creation, I see that as the Light of the Holy Spirit. When the War breaks out, the Holy

Spirit would have been in the universe (if not the Garden). Where is the Wilderness then?

Big question.

It could be someplace on earth or it could be out in the outer recesses of the Universe. A curious word used in about half of the twenty English translations I looked at was "they" nourished her. The only reference possible for this pronoun happens to be stars. Could the two-thirds of the remaining angels rally behind the Woman (Holy Spirit)? The Christ just vanished, so who is Satan able to war against?

Before we get to the war, I think it's important to look at the time mentioned: one thousand two hundred and sixty days. That is pretty specific. Daniel brings up some very similar times during his End Times prophecies. Later in Revelation, the Two Witnesses will prophesy in Jerusalem for exactly 1260 days. Add those days up and they equal about 3 ½ years, which seems to be about the same time. Time, Times, and ½ a Time could also be seen as Time=1 year, and thus 3 ½ years (or is this symbolic and nebulous).

Why such specific times?

I think for John (and us) to understand God's symbolic times that will be used in the End Times, we needed to understand what happened way back in the beginning. In other words, God is going to honor what happened in the Beginning by repeating it again in the End.

So Satan leaves the Garden…and then what? How long does it take to rally the angels? How long does he organize? How long does he have to search for the Woman? How long until we have angel vs. angel? This 1260 days and Time, Times, and Half-a-

Time could be overlaid or butted against each other. My point is that it is a history lesson about the length of this conflict from antiquity.

Section D: The War

[Revelation 12:7] And there was war in heaven: Michael and his angels fought against the dragon; and the dragon fought and his angels, 8 And prevailed not; neither was their place found any more in heaven. 9And the great dragon was cast out, that old serpent, called the Devil, and Satan, which deceiveth the whole world: he was cast out into the earth, and his angels were cast out with him.

As an English teacher, those adjective and appositive clauses and phrases drove me nuts, but John just wanted to clarify that what he saw was all about Satan. But it is the WHEN that interests me.

Luke 10:18 is the verse where Jesus references that He was there from the beginning and that he saw Satan fall from Heaven as lightning. So our Section D seems to be history. Certainly, Satan could try to take Heaven again and this is a double-veiled prophecy concerning the past and future, but let's analyze it as a flashback. Jesus seems to confirm Satan's fall as history.

If Satan could not find the Woman (the Holy Spirit) then he would take the fight to Heaven, where Michael and his angels were protecting the Child. Did it take them 1259 days of fighting to get to this point? Was the war waged on both Heaven and Earth? It doesn't really say. We do know what happened.

Satan got his head busted!

In <u>Luke 10:18</u>, I think Jesus plays it coy. Satan had reached Heaven! Strategically, this war was almost over if he had reached Heaven and/or the Throne. Who threw him out? Michael? Psalm 74 talks poetically about the broken heads of Leviathan. Isaiah 27 and 51 also mention it. Job 41 talks about the Leviathan as the "king of the children of pride." We just heard John talk about Satan as a dragon. In Revelation 13, we hear about the Dragon having a wounded head.

When did he get his head wounded?

We need to double back to the Genesis <u>3:15</u> prophecy:

[Genesis 3:15]. And I will put enmity between thee and the woman, and between thy seed and her seed; it shall bruise thy head, and thou shalt bruise his heel.

Juxtaposing these two chapters makes you question the "woman" definition, but let's look at the order of wounding. Notice how Jesus first bruises the head of Satan? Then Satan will bruise Jesus's heel. I think this is reason why Psalms and Isaiah mention it ***prior*** to the Easter story actually happening. Satan and Company didn't get their butts kicked, they got their heads kicked—by the Christ.

Section E: How the War was Won.

[Revelation 12:10-12]. Then I heard a loud voice saying in heaven, And I heard a loud voice saying in heaven, Now is come salvation, and strength, and the kingdom of our God, and the power of his Christ: for the accuser of our brethren is cast down, which accused them before our God day and night. 11 And they overcame him by the blood of the Lamb, and by the word of their testimony; and they loved not their lives unto

the death. 12 Therefore rejoice, ye heavens, and ye that dwell in them. Woe to the inhabiters of the earth and of the sea! for the devil is come down unto you, having great wrath, because he knoweth that he hath but a short time.

Still a flashback.

For years, I hastily read past this section just because it seems to be a big long celebration. The war was over, hurray! First of all, let's look at who is celebrating. Not God. Not the Christ. The only obvious choice is Michael and/or the angels. They are celebrating Satan's defeat. Now remember that they'd been fighting him for 1260 days (day and night) before the war ended. They were happy it was over, but more importantly, they were happy with HOW it ended.

(This part is really strange.)

At the beginning of this chapter, I listed a bunch of Old Testament celebrities who seemed to "get it." The promise of the Christ was handed down through these generations because they seemed to show/earn it. The angel mentioned "brethren" or "brothers" or "buddies" in this verse. Remember, it was Satan who accused humans of not being worthy, and then a war broke out. From what I can tell, Adam and Eve were the only humans mentioned in early Genesis, so the accuser of our brethren becomes literally the accuser of Adam and Eve or symbolically the accuser of humanity. Humanity was on the line when Satan smashed in the doors of Heaven to kill the Christ (who changed the Status Quo).

Yes, the "power of His Christ" is credited for Satan's defeat, but the parts after it intrigue me. After 1260 days, what suddenly turned the tide of war? Adam and Eve.

Imagine the guilt of Adam and Eve as not only their status quo changes but so too does all of creation. Now toss in a war. While they hunkered down for three and a half years, they must have been filled with regret, anger, loss, more anger, and as is the case with most humans, denial of responsibility.

And the war raged on.

Think about how you wrestle with your own sins. Now try to imagine how Adam and Eve struggled during those 1260 days. Adam blamed Eve. Eve blamed the Serpent. As the only humans, they could have gone to their graves bitter and angry, which explains the line **"they did not love their lives to the death."** If Adam and Eve refused to "pass it on" by having children. If Adam and Eve refused to "pass it on" by even believing in the prophecy of "fixing it" (which is the prophecy of the coming Christ).

And the war raged on.

But at some time during those terrible early days, Adam and Eve came to a realization. They stopped feeling and found their faith. They overcame Satan. They believed in the **"blood of the Lamb."** They were responsible for helping to win this war by their testimony. These two fallen humans were reborn in a way. They might have been filled with the Holy Spirit. Just like the sinner King David fought through all of his vices to believe in the coming Christ, so too did Adam and Eve.

And Satan got kicked in the head.

This angelic celebration quickly turned into a warning.

Section F: The Warning.

So Satan spit at her?

Jerk move, if you ask me. In fact, this section gets so epic and hyperbolic it is hard to understand what is even happening. Did Satan just try to destroy all life on the planet? Did this bully just try to murder Adam and Eve also? If Light=Life=Holy Spirit, I think Satan tried to use his powers to return the planet back to the status quo of Day One. Is this a prequel to the Great Flood of Noah? It is curious that Satan's powers were immediately thwarted by the planet itself. It is as if God reminded Satan who wrote the Physics book. You want to get paranormal, Satan? Snap! No more water.

Satan was having a really bad day.

In this section, you can also see a little more support on how I think the woman is an entity like the Holy Spirit. Neither Eve nor Mary sprouted wings and flapped away to safety. This is also perplexing if it is Israel or the Church. But if this is the Holy Spirit, then the wings make sense. It would also make sense how Jesus promised the return of the Holy Spirit to the Christians of the Pentecost. How could the Holy Spirit make a glorious appearance if it hadn't gone "into the wilderness."?

Unable to destroy the Christ (who just kicked his head) or the Woman (who just vanished), Satan was left to make war on the enlightened believers. The entirety of the Old Testament seems to be God-fearing believers getting hammered by Satan.

Exhibit A: Job.

Adam and Eve, Abraham, Moses, King David, and (pick a prophet) all did their part to keep the anachronistic **"testimony of Jesus Christ,"** which meant they did not love their lives to the death but instead believed in the promise of his coming.

CHAPTER THREE

MARY, MARY

The mystery of Mary has existed almost as long as Christianity. Who was this woman that gave birth to the Christ? Why was she chosen? What would her life have been like? What happened to her later in life?

The Gospels only scratch the surface of answering our questions, and as a result, there are all sorts of theories and traditions that have collected through two millennia. Before we get to Luke's account, let's take a look at some of the other sources for information about Mary.

In Chapter One, I brought up the two genealogies of Jesus. The early church historian Eusebius cited another scholar by the name of Africanus, who offered a theory. After connecting "grandpa" Jacob and Heli as brothers, Eusebius claimed that Mary would have belonged to the same tribe as Joseph based on Mosaic laws concerning intertribal marriage. With this theory, Mary is also in the line of King David, and thus the lists, despite not mentioning her, would also be her family tree (of sorts).

There must also be a bit of skepticism about the absolute nature of this Mosaic Law. Things rarely go according to the letter of the law. After all, we have all sorts of "tainted" blood mentioned in the story of the Scarlet Thread, so being of the House of David can only be seen as probable.

There are actually two "apocryphal" books that came out of the early Christian church that add all sorts of lore to Mary's story. Before I explain, I have to be clear about what an apocryphal book is. If you flip on the History Channel, you often hear about the "Lost Books of the Bible" as if something hidden or missing has been suddenly discovered. This might not be the case.

Canon vs. Fodder

Let's talk about the "canon" first. The Bible as we know it today has "pretty much" had the same books since Constantine allowed the Christian Church to come out of the shadows. To crudely summarize the complicated events of the time, Emperor Constantine wanted to understand what it meant to be a Christian. One of the byproducts of this era was a "canon" of books that the church fathers felt every Christian should know. Centuries later, reformation scholars like Luther disputed a couple of books that didn't really include any "God" messages (like Maccabees) and suggested to downgrade them to just being "apocryphal."

Thus a secondary level of religious texts are considered to be "apocryphal." Along with all of the texts Luther felt were "legit" but not really worthy of the "canon" were many older books that existed back in the time of Constantine. These apocryphal books were not included for a variety of reasons. Some were simply not divinely inspired. Some of them were widely read by a certain region but not by another, who saw them as too foreign. Others simply had "origin" issues where there was too much uncertainty about translation or authorship. As a result, these books were read by scholars but not distributed to the churches.

A little bit lower in reverence were the "pseudepigraphal" texts. These books meant "falsely ascribed." In other words, these books have serious authorship issues. Either the author was anonymous or it was ascribed to someone who could not have written it. In many cases, these historic books had the "phone tree" issue where there were too many variations on the texts to ever be able to determine which one was the "legit" version. Some New Testament letters include references to some of these texts.

The worst type of text (in my view) are the Gnostic texts. These are the texts that the cable television shows often dresses up as "Christian" texts when they are anything but. The Gnostics were a dangerous threat to the early church that affected them as early as the Book of Acts (Simon the Magus) and as late as the Book of Revelation (the Nicolaitans). The Gnostics used the names of Christian leaders and put Christian labels on a religion that was heretical and contrary to the teachings of Jesus. This threat even existed in the time of forming the cannon, which is why it was important to define Christianity (so you knew if you were being duped).

Early Accounts of Mary

So there are two ancient texts (***The Gospel of the Birth of Mary*** & ***The Protevangellion of James)*** that were read and known by early church fathers but not included in the Bible. I assumed there were good reasons not to continue to hand them down through the generations. Even though these two books are not considered to be "Gospel," they were certainly interesting to take a peek at.

Why peek?

There are many traditional ideas about Christmas that still exist that cannot be found in the Gospels. Do you picture Joseph as an older man? Does your Christmas card involve beams of light and a cave? Do your Wise Men go to a house in Bethlehem? If yes, where did you get these ideas?

The Gospel of the Birth of Mary is an old text passed around in Christian churches that was attributed to Matthew (doesn't mean it was ***that*** Matthew). It existed in the 4th century and could be found by many religious scholars of the time. Even though it didn't become canon, early church fathers like St. Jerome knew of it, whether it was seen favorably or utterly dismissed.

The Gospel of the Birth of Mary tells that Mary came from the House of David instead of being from the House of Levi (Levite=high priest material). It does include a similar angel announcement but to Mary's parents, who were told she would bear the Christ. Because of this, Mary was sent to the Temple and was allowed to visit the Holiest of Holies (flagrant violation of code/laws…sigh). She was allowed this because she miraculously floated up the temple stairs as a sign of her divine stamp of approval. While in the Temple, she was prepped for her role by the Ark (yes, it was still there???) until the day Joseph arrived (well advanced in years) and won her hand in a strange contest that is reminiscent of drawing straws (their shepherd staffs). From betrothal, Joseph takes her to Nazareth, where she conceives the Christ. It also clearly says how Joseph **never** had sex with her then or later in the marriage.

Again, I include this story not to claim it as right or wrong but to simply show you where some very old traditions find their roots.

The Protevangelium of James is another apocryphal book believed to be written about the year AD 145. Which James wrote it? The James that was beheaded early in the book of Acts? The James who was considered the "Brother" of Jesus, also known as James the Just? Didn't he die in Jerusalem (Jerusalem was destroyed in 70 AD)? Some other James? Ah…now do you see why it is considered apocryphal? Along with the authorship issues, there were multiple problems in the text that didn't jive with custom or scripture. So we are left with an 1,800 year old account of Mary that may or may not be accurate.

Let's peek.

Early on, we learn that Mary's parents were a rich man named Joachim and a barren woman named Anna. After fasting and prayer, and angel announces that they will have an important child, Mary, who is then educated by angels in the Temple.

Later, when she is older, there is a strange competition for her hand in marriage. Ultimately, an old widower by the name of Joseph had a dove burst from his staff and land on his head that signified that he was selected to be Mary's husband.

The story continues, and adds the visit by Gabriel, who spoke out of a pitcher of water. In this account, Joseph returns from a building project to find Mary six months pregnant.

Annas the High Priest then brings both Mary and Joseph to trial, which ultimately ends with drinking magic poison water, which reveals she was speaking the truth.

Just before the birth, the decree is made involving registering in Bethlehem. So Joseph complains about registering all of his sons (like James, Joses, Simon, and Jude) along with Mary. They travel through a desert, and upon arriving in Bethlehem, find a cave for the birth.

Instead of giving birth the traditional way, a bright cloud wraps around Mary, and with the help of a midwife named Salome, poof…Jesus.

In this version, the magi show up in Bethlehem, causing commotion, and gaining Herod's attention, who sent them right back to Bethlehem so he could learn the location of the Christ. In this version, a single bright star shone so brightly that none of the other stars could be seen, and that allowed them to find the cave, where this really bright star stood upon.

Just like in the Gospel account, there was a warning, but this version has Mary receiving the warning. At this point, she hid him in a manger in an ox-stall. Elizabeth, who apparently lives in Bethlehem, also hides baby John by commanding the mountain to hide her and the baby John. Unfortunately, Zacharias is murdered by Herod's troops at the stairs of the temple, and is replaced by Simeon.

Wow.

It is both awesome yet so wrong at the same time.

Gospel Accounts of Mary

Now that we've looked at some of the "lore" sources for Mary, let's look at the details that Luke gives in his gospel.

[Luke 1:26] Now in the 6th month, the angel Gabriel was sent by God to a city of Galilee named Nazareth to a virgin betrothed to a man whose name was Joseph, of the house of David. The virgin's name was Mary.

The first thing to notice is that this is the same angel sent to Zacharias and Elizabeth six months earlier. If Zacharias was serving in the Holiest of Holies for his encounter, John was conceived around our September. Here we are, six months later, when Mary is about to conceive, which puts us around March— almost the Passover. I bring this up now in order to argue the birthdate later (yes, nine months after March will be December).

You should know that Nazareth was not an ancient town like Jerusalem or even Bethlehem. Nazareth was a "workers" town that was filled with Jews who worked for various Roman/Herod building projects in the area. As a result, it earned the same reputation as the towns in our old west (or even modern North Dakota). It was not known for being anything close to fanatic (or even very religious).

Another strange thing to note in this opening section is how well did Mary and Joseph know each other? How long did they know each other?

I've read (I think it is even in Leviticus) that good Jewish young people were encouraged to marry within their tribes.

While this might be a bit strange to us, it probably helped maintain tribal identity. However, at this time, the northern tribes had almost vanished into the wind, leaving the tribes of Judah, Benjamin, and Levi as the most dominant tribes. So most teens in those days didn't really have issues "keeping it within the tribe." King David came from the tribe of Judah (specifically in Bethlehem) but by this time, most Jews living in Galilee or Judea were from the tribe of Judah.

Does this mean Mary also came from the line of David? Or was she just another Jew from the tribe of Judah. One question that I have about this section is: what was a Davidic Jew doing in Nazareth? In a little bit, we'll see Joseph identify Bethlehem as his hometown, so does that mean he'd only recently gone to Bethlehem? Had his family been there for a hundred years or for two years? What caused somebody from a branch of the "royal" family to migrate so far north from home?

[Luke 1:28] And the angel came in unto her, and said, Hail, thou that art highly favoured, the Lord is with thee: blessed art thou among women.

This single verse is where the idea of the Immaculate Conception originates. Mary won the lottery ticket. Gabriel showed up to announce she'd won the prize. Her womb would bring the Christ into the world. The Immaculate Conception doesn't just mean that Mary was a virgin (aka immaculate). The official dogma means that Mary was without sin.

Is this stretching "the LORD is with thee" too far?

Can "highly favored" actually mean sinless?

From just Luke, this argument is a bit tenuous, but if you look back at the lore, the divine nature of Mary is embedded into both the *Gospel of the Birth of Mary* and the *Protevangeli-um* accounts. It wasn't until 1854 with Pope Pius IX that it was officially asserted that Mary did not carry original sin.

Sound too Catholic? Well, read what Luther wrote about the issue: "Mary is full of grace, proclaimed to be entirely without sin. God's grace fills her with everything good and makes her devoid of all evil. God is with her, meaning that all she did or left undone is divine and the action of God is in her. Moreover, God guided and protected her from all that might be hurtful to her."

Regardless of how you feel about this issue, one thing is pretty clear: Mary was special. Humanity had waited since the days of Adam and Eve for the fulfillment of God's promise, and finally, Gabriel showed up to tell her she was the one.

[Luke 1:29] And when she saw him, she was troubled at his saying, and cast in her mind what manner of salutation this should be. [30] And the angel said unto her, Fear not, Mary: for thou hast found favour with God. [31] And, behold, thou shalt conceive in thy womb, and bring forth a son, and shalt call his name JESUS.

I love Mary's humility in her reaction. Perhaps it is pretty scary for Gabriel to visit you, but look at how she doesn't give him any backtalk (compared to Zacharias). She doesn't question. She doesn't say, "but, but, but…" She simply accepts it.

Dang!

She certainly was troubled (concerned/freaked out). After all, she was a betrothed virgin about to be pregnant—that's big trouble! When she reflects on the manner of the greeting, it makes it seem as if she understands the BIG PICTURE (which

Zacharias didn't) instead of her personal concerns. That's how you win the lottery, I guess.

If you wanted to argue against the Immaculate Conception idea, then verse 30 could give you support. Instead of being born or destined, Gabriel declares that she has "found" favor with God. This slightly implies that it was something to be searched for or discovered. After being found, **then** Gabriel arrives.

Splitting hairs.

There is another curious word that has a dramatic impact on how you read the passage. It is a future tense word: will.

You will conceive.

In other words, this is not a pregnancy stick moment with a plus or a minus. Gabriel is not there to give Mary a high-five and congrats. Gabriel is there telling her what will happen in her near future.

[Luke 1:32] He shall be great, and shall be called the Son of the Highest: and the Lord God shall give unto him the throne of his father David: [33] And he shall reign over the house of Jacob for ever; and of his kingdom there shall be no end.

Well, if Mary wasn't certain, she is now. This wasn't just going to be a miracle baby like John the Baptist. She was going to give birth to the Son of God. The divine would be made flesh. Yet the second half must have given her real pause. Gabriel mentions how Jesus would also get the throne of David and rule over Israel (which at the time was mostly just Judah) Instead of divine prophecy, she gets a prophecy involving the physical world (just not in her lifetime). This leads her to ask a few important questions.

[Luke 1:34] Then Mary said to the angel, 'How can this be, seeing I know not a man?

Mary is fairly pragmatic here. She admits a basic biological problem. She hasn't had sex (like Zacharias and Elizabeth) for her miracle to happen. Or perhaps she is admitting hereditary issue. Does this mean she is **not** an heir of David? If she had first married David, then this promise would have been quite obvious and easy. The son of Joseph had a claim to the crown. Did Mary? Is that why she asked her question?

Overshadowed

[Luke 1:35] And the angel answered and said to her, 'The Holy Ghost will come upon you, and the power of the Highest will overshadow you; therefore, also that holy thing which shall be born of thee shall be called the Son of God.

1. The Holy Ghost
1. The Highest
1. Son of God

1+1+1=3. Are you kidding me? Earlier, I mentioned how Gabriel was speaking about the future. In this verse, the future tense is used three times. If you are picturing a beam of light through a window, or Mary touching her belly to feel a flutter— hold the press! Gabriel is prepping her for something that is about to happen—and it's really big: the Trinity.

Before you go and picture Mary in her bed at night, next to a well, or walking in a field, let's take a trip back in time to review a similar moment.

Now, according to John's Gospel, twice, "no one has ever seen God." Despite all the other appearances in the Old Testament, John clarifies that no one but Jesus has ever really seen the actual God. The closest moment I can think of is Moses. Remember him going up to the top of Mount Horeb (Sinai)? Before going to the pinnacle, he put rocks around the circumference of the mountain so that none of the Hebrews would get too close and drop dead. Why would they drop dead? Because they were too full of sin to stand in the presence of God. That is quite a big "safe zone."

Moses also had to brace himself so that the violence of the encounter didn't sweep him away. Even the Hebrews below asked Moses to speak to God because they were too afraid to hear God themselves.

That's how scary this moment was.

That was just the presence of God.

According to Gabriel, the Holy Spirit would soon come upon her. According to Gabriel, the Highest was coming to overshadow Mary. Remember what happened when God "overshadowed" Moses? He ended up glowing! Not only that, but the Christ, who has existed since the beginning, (and perhaps was the face of God in the OT) was going to be there also.

This wasn't congratulation.

This was a warning.

<u>With Haste</u>

Now, I stopped in the middle of Gabriel's speech, which lasted less than a minute. Gabriel continued to say:

[Luke 1:36] And, behold, thy cousin Elisabeth, she hath also conceived a son in her old age: and this is the sixth month with her, who was called barren. [37] For with God nothing shall be

impossible. [38] And Mary said, Behold the handmaid of the Lord; be it unto me according to thy word. And the angel departed from her. [39] And Mary arose in those days, and went into the hill country with haste…

It is verse 39 that so intrigues me. As soon as the angel departs, Mary leaves. Different English translations use different words like "hurried," "instantly," and "hurriedly," which seems to universally imply "left quickly."

Did she tell others? Did she pack? Did she wait for a caravan? Did she wait for her whole family to leave for the Passover? I don't have answers for those questions, but I do know she left in a hurry. Why would she leave in a hurry?

If this "Trinity" moment happened while she was still in Nazareth, what would have happened? First, it would not have been discreet. When God showed up for Moses, it scared the tar out of the Hebrews far below in the valley. It was a light show. Plus, Nazareth already had a reputation of being an ungodly town. If the conception happened in town, this could have endangered lives. People would have dropped dead just by being too close to Mary when God visited her.

So the departing "immediately" aspect is revealing, but where she went is also important.

The town of Nazareth is strategically located. To the north, there were thriving Roman centers that fed the economy. Just to the west, the King's Highway provided an ancient route from Egypt to Damascus. This road, along the flat coastal lands, allowed a fairly quick trip to Judea and Jerusalem. To the east, Nazareth connected to a mountain range that acted as a spine that paralleled the Jordan River all the way south.

So verse 39 gives a bit of an idea the route Mary took to get there: she went straight south and stayed in the mountains. To me, this seems to eliminate both the caravan idea and the family trip idea. This route was harder and longer. In the mountains (or hill country), she was able to covertly travel the 70 miles or so to wherever Elizabeth lived.

So we have her route, but the one thing that isn't explained is when did the "Trinity" moment happen? When did conception happen? When she shows up in Judea a few days later, Elizabeth and Prenatal John know the Christ is inside Mary.

The Valley of Megiddo

If it didn't happen in Nazareth, and it was done by the time she got to Judea, it had to happen somewhere along the way. I believe she needed isolation. The vague "hill country" would certainly provide that. It is easy to explain the phrase "hill country" as Judea, the entire mountain range, or the hills around Nazareth. Or perhaps it is just the opposite of obvious (the flat roads). However, sandwiched between two foothills, is a place that might have guaranteed isolation: the Valley of Megiddo.

Yes, the famed Armageddon location is just below the hill where Nazareth is built. Today, it is a flat, fertile agricultural area. Back then, it was shunned. In previous centuries, the Valley of Megiddo was an evil place where thousands of soldiers lost their lives on the battlefield (see Josiah or Ezekiel 37). Jews really did their best to avoid the place.

In the future, this is also the location where Jesus will return to defeat the armies of the Antichrist. Epic spot, huh?

So what (and this is a stretch) if…this is where the Christ came into our world? Was it on the way to Judea? Certainly. Would it have been isolated? Yes. Does it hold symbolic significance? Yep. Is there anything else between there and Judea on par with it? Nope.

Now, I also like to think Mary had a "predestination" sort of confidence after this "Trinity" moment that would have allowed a young woman to confidently know she'd get there safe. It SHALL BE. Mary knew she'd give birth. What did she fear?

CHAPTER FOUR

QUITE CONTRARY: THE OTHER MARY

Again, if you want to jump right into the Christmas story, skip ahead a bit, because now that we've talked about Mary, I want to talk a bit more about the family situation of both Mary and Joseph. If you focus just on the traditional Christmas texts, there is only ONE Mary, but by the time you get to the Easter story, there are bunches. It was during my study and dissection of these Easter texts that I sorted out (in my mind, at least) who these different Mary's were.

How to start?

Oh, Brothers

Let's jump ahead three decades. Imagine Jesus is ministering and touring the Holy Lands with his disciples. During this tour, he encounters people who "knew him when." These people that knew Him before the ministry years seem taken aback (not because of a Saul/Paul character transformation) because modest Jesus comes from modest origins.

> **[Matthew 13:55] Whence hath this man this wisdom, and these mighty works? [55] Is not this the carpenter's son? is not his mother called Mary? and his brethren (brothers), James, and Joses, and Simon, and Judas (Jude)? [56] And his sisters, are they not all with us?**

To rephrase, somebody said, "Hey I know this guy's family," in order to try to diminish Jesus OR because the divine nature he saw contrasts the very human nature of the rest of the family.

In the previous chapter, you read two old accounts of the origins of Mary, which referenced Joseph as an old man with sons (assumedly from a previous marriage), Regardless of where you stand on the validity of those two accounts, Matthew opens up a whole can of worms with his verse.

First, ask yourself if Joseph is alive during Jesus' ministry? How old do you picture him in the Nativity? This passage almost mentions him in the present tense as if he is still alive. We'll get back to Joseph later.

Next, it obviously points out that Mary is his mother. To help clarify things, I will give Mary the last name of Joachim so we can later clarify all of our Marys. According to both the legends and the Catholic Church, Mary Joachim only had Jesus. Other Christian denominations boldly claim these children mentioned here in 13:55 as younger brothers and sisters of Jesus because it seems natural and regular for husband and wife to have more children.

This point can be endlessly debated in theory.

Some people will explain that brothers=brethren=disciples so that Mary and Joseph can continue to have only 1 son.

Could be.

However, when I read Acts 1:12, it lists each disciple (including James Alphaeus, Simon the Zealot, and Judas the son of James) but *then* also talks about **"the women and Mary the mother of Jesus (Mary J), and (H)is brothers."** Mark 3:31 (as well as Matt 12 and Luke 8) also seem to strongly juxtapose brothers against disciples:

> **[Mark 3:31] There came then his brethren and his mother, and, standing without, sent unto him, calling him. [32] And the multitude sat about him, and they said unto him, Behold, thy mother and thy brethren without seek for thee. [33] And he answered them, saying, Who is my mother, or my brethren? [34] And he looked round about on them which sat about him, and said, Behold my mother and my brethren! [35] For whosoever shall do the will of God, the same is my brother, and my sister, and mother.**

There are a couple of other verses that seem to pile on the sibling idea, but instead of ignoring them, let's take a look. Later in Jesus' ministry, things become a bit dangerous, especially in Jerusalem. Since this is a Christmas story, I'll move past the shady nature of the anecdote to just give the lines about his brothers:

> **[John 7:1] After these things Jesus walked in Galilee: for he would not walk in Jewry (Judea), because the Jews sought to kill him. [2] Now the Jews' feast of tabernacles was at hand. 3 His brethren therefore said unto him, Depart hence, and go into Judaea, that thy disciples also may see the works that thou doest. [4] For there is no man that doeth any thing in secret,**

and he himself seeketh to be known openly. If thou do these things, shew thyself to the world. [5] For neither did his brethren believe in him. [6] Then Jesus said unto them, My time is not yet come: but your time is alway ready. [7] The world cannot hate you; but me it hateth, because I testify of it, that the works thereof are evil. [8] Go ye up unto this feast: I go not up yet unto this feast; for my time is not yet full come. [9] When he had said these words unto them, he abode still in Galilee.

Again and again, it seems to imply actual brothers of Jesus; however, I am not quite ready to accept that Mary had several children. As a Lutholicatist, I want to reconcile everything rather than cast stones at one of the glass houses.

What are our choices, though?

A. "Brothers" do not mean siblings.

B. Mary and Joseph had children after Jesus was born.

C. Joseph had a previous wife who died and left him with children.

D. None of the above.

I'm going with D, so bear with me a while longer. First, let's go back to a point from an earlier chapter.

Uncle Clopas Theory

Do you remember the boring name list given by "Legal Luke" and "Biological Matthew," and how it differed as early as Jesus's grandfather? Was it Heli or Jacob? Tradition says his maternal grandfather was Joachim. Let's establish an old Hebrew custom found in Genesis. Judah had a son named Er and a daughter-in-law named Tamar. When Er died, he was legally obliged to let Onan provide her with a son (things got complicated after that). My point is, when you have two brothers, and a brother dies childless, the surviving brother has to take her as a wife (or...) if the brother died with children, the wife and the children become the "son of" the brother. Yes, it seems strange to us but it was a general welfare, legal, inheritance issue back then. If grandpa Jacob died, then Joseph became the "son of Heli" even though he was genetically the son of Jacob.

Since older brothers usually die first because of age, this legal shift probably happened a lot. When Luke wrote his account, he just went with Grandpa Heli because...you know...law stuff. Matthew, who might have known more because he was a local boy, might have known Joseph's biological father was Jacob and traced the bloodline for the points he was making. Both were right.

So what if Joseph had an older brother?

In the strictest Gospel reading, there obviously only seems to be Mary, Joseph, and baby Jesus at the manger (and the sheep, too). Where are the older brothers from another mother? Again, you could theorize and answer but in the Christmas story, there is no support.

Thirty year time jump...

The Other Women

Jesus is now hanging on the cross. All disciples but one have split. It is safe for the women to go near the cross (sexist Romans) as well as a disciple that either has a magical golden ticket or is so young they don't see him as a threat (age-biased Romans)…the Beloved Disciple, John. John stood at the cross, and when he later wrote about what happened, he included names:

[John 19:25] But there stood by the cross of Jesus his mother (Mary Joachim), **and his mother's sister, Mary the wife of Cleophas** (Clopas), **and Mary Magdalene."**

Was that an appositive phrase within a list? How many women did you count? 3 or 4? Oh boy, roll up your sleeves, this is going to get a bit messy.

Woman #A: Mary Joachim, his mother.

Woman #B: Mary Magdalene, right?

Woman #C: His mother's sister, Mary the wife of Clopas or…

Woman #C: His mother's sister, which could mean…

Woman #D: Mary the wife of Clopas.

Come on, John. Why did you have to mess up this list? Let's see if the other disciples added any clarity when they gave their lists.

[Mark 15:40] There were also women looking on afar off: among whom was Mary Magdalene (B), **and Mary the mother of James the less and of Joses** (A? C? D?), **and Salome (C? D?)** and later at the tomb…
"Mary Magdalene (B) **and Mary the mother of Joses** (A? C? D?) **saw where His body was laid.**

That made it worse!

[Matthew 27:56]: Among which was Mary Magdalene (B), **and Mary the mother of James and Joseph** (A? C? D?) **and the mother of Zebedee's sons** (C? D? E?)

And later at the burial 27:61:

And there was Mary Magdalene (B) and the other Mary (???) sitting over against the sepulchre.

At Easter morning:

[Matt 28:1] In the end of the Sabbath, as it began to dawn toward the first day of the week, came Mary Magdalene and the other Mary to see the sepulcher.

Luke also includes a list a bit later.

[Luke 24:10] It was Mary Magdalene (B), and Joanna (??), and Mary the mother of James (A? C? D?), and other women (??) that were with them, which told these things unto the apostles."

Clear as mud?

Just James

To help clarify the women, let's clarify the men first, starting with James. There are three prominent Jameses. James the son of Zebedee is the older brother of John, the Beloved Disciple. This James is one of the 12 disciples. This James is one of the fab four that Jesus often has special moments with. He is the first disciple to die as a martyr in the book of Acts when he is beheaded.

The next guy is James the son of Alpheus. This is another of the twelve disciples. He does not get a lot of Biblical playing time.

The third guy is James O'Mikros (neither a last name or Irish). Mark mentions James O'Mikros when he says his mother was at the cross **"Mary the mother of James the Less."** Now, you could speculate that James Zebedee is "famous James" and James the Less could be O'Mikros, but the term does not mean unimportant but instead "small." Galatians 1:19 eliminates this James as a disciple but instead adds that he was **"the Lord's brother."** This third James later becomes a major player in the Book of Acts (Acts 14) and in church history as James the Just or James the Righteous.

Okay, I'm ready to make my turn on this complicated point. Clopas!

The wife of Clopas is key, but John is the only one to mention him. Who was Clopas?

I am going to explain why Option D: None of the Above fits the best. I think Clopas was the brother of Joseph and UNCLE of Jesus.

Support: I'm going with three women and an appositive. When John says **"But there stood by the cross of Jesus his mother** (Mary Joachim), **and his mother's sister, Mary the wife of Cleophas** (Clopas), **and Mary Magdalene"** he knew there were three Marys.

Sister-By-Law

Sister Mary: Now it is really, really improbable that Joachim and Anna had a baby girl named Mary and then later named another daughter Mary, because…you know…weird. However, if Uncle Clopas died, his wife would become the "welfare" wife of Joseph and the "sister-in-law" of Mary Joachim (Instead of polygamy, think of it as cultural welfare).

Mrs. Zebedee: I've heard many theories that Jesus was the cousin of James and John, the sons of Zebedee. I get that the previous pages are confusing and arguments can easily be made.

The wife of Zebedee was there. The mother of James was also there.

Brothers of Jesus	Children of Zebedee
James	James
Joses	John
Simon	
Jude	

Matthew 27 can certainly support this "Cousin John" theory, but it really doesn't fit with the rest of the story. Remember the baptism? James, John, and Andrew all rush to Peter to announce they've found the Christ. Wouldn't cousins already know each other? Theory dropped (for me).

Aunt Mary Amram: Again, if John uses an appositive phrase to clarify which of the three Mary's he is talking about, it reads: **and his mother's sister, Mary the wife of Clopas.** Aunt Mary is not biologically related. It says "sister" but it means "aunt." Joachim did not name two daughters Mary. Uncle Clopas met and married a young woman named Mary (Amram), and later, his brother Joseph married a different woman named Mary (Joachim).

The Firstborn Son

How the theory works: Imagine you are in Nazareth. You want to build a new house. Need a carpenter? Great. You're in luck. It just so happens that Heli and Sons Carpentry have some of the best carpenters around. The eldest son (who would one day inherit the business) is Clopas. He's been groomed (just like Peter for fishing, and James for whatever Zebedee does) to take over the business as the oldest son. He's wealthy and already has a growing family with his wife (Mary of Amram) and children (James, Joses, Simon, Jude, daughter, daughter, etc.).

The younger brother Joseph will not inherit the business. He is not wealthy and probably has a hard time saving up money for a bride/dowry. He might even need to find a new vocation one day. Remember the lot of the second son? (Andrew became a religious trainee to John the Baptist, and John the Disciple became a religious trainee as well). The second son either joins the church or gets a new career. Joseph knows carpentry but probably begins a study of scripture.

During the Nativity timeline, Uncle Clopas and Aunt Mary simply keep-on keeping-on up in Nazareth. They might have some or all of the "siblings" listed in Matt 13:55. Their children (James, Joses, Simon, and Jude) will one day be cousins of Christ.

Nice theory, but is there support?

Yes.

Cousins of Christ

When I began to research James the Just (O'Mikros), I first came across the stories written by the Jewish historian Josephus. James the Just was a double-agent leader of both the Jewish and Christian faiths. This is why Paul and Peter asked him for a ruling in <u>Acts 14:4</u>. Paul later talks about him in <u>Galatians 1:19</u> when he says, **"But other of the apostles saw I none, save James the Lord's brother."** (Apostle=follower, not disciple). James the son of Zebedee is dead. This is not James Alpheus either. This is James the Just, the Lord's brother. This is the same guy who wrote the book of James, Later, James the Just is killed on the Passover for not betraying the Christians by denouncing Jesus. Martyr!

Two early church writers also added some clarification for this theory. Hegisippus (110-180) explained that Clopas was the brother of Joseph. In this explanation, he described how Simon followed his brother James as Bishop of Jerusalem and that both were cousins of Jesus. While I really like this theory, he claims that Clopas is the younger brother who becomes the foster-father of Jesus (The Carpenter's son?).

Papias, the Bishop of Hierapolis (70-110) wrote that Simon was a cousin of Jesus as was the brother of James the Just, who died at the age of 120 around 70 AD. (when the Temple was destroyed). In this case, James is almost 50 when Jesus was born, meaning Clopas had to be a LOT older than Joseph. James is NOT a disciple but acts as the mediator between Paul and Peter. Remember the other brother? Well, Jude became the author of Jude, who claims to be the brother of James.

So when you hear about the Other Mary, Mary's Sister, the Wife of Clopas, the Mother of James the Less and Joses, the Mother of James…this is Mary, the Daughter of Amram. She is the wife of Clopas. She is Aunt Mary.

Now, the reason to bring up all of these names is not just to give you a headache but also to show that the family structure of Jesus could have been a lot more complicated than your basic nativity set portrays. Having an Aunt and Uncle as well as cousins really will complicate matters later on.

Were the cousins jealous of the wonder-baby Jesus?

Did something bad happen to Clopas while Jesus was growing up?

How did the extended family react to all of the strange things that Mary and Joseph were about to do after Gabriel showed up?

CHAPTER FIVE

A MESSAGE ABOUT MESSENGERS

The arrival of Jesus did not just come out of the blue. This was not a fanatical movement created by the oppressive Roman occupiers. The Christ prophecy was the "fix" to an older problem—sin. It began when Adam, Eve, and Satan were lined up in the Garden while receiving their punishments.

Enochian lore also predicted a messiah that would save mankind. After the flood, Abraham took the prophetic baton, bringing more focus and clarity to the coming Christ. Then Jacob took the baton from Esau, and by the time the Hebrews came out of Israel, King David and the prophets brought specific purpose and definition to the Christ.

One of the more interesting turns that the Christ prophecy took was the idea that he would be preceded by another divinely ordained messenger that would prepare the way.

[Mark 1:2] As it is written in the prophets, Behold, I send my messenger before thy face, which shall prepare thy way before thee. [3] The voice of one crying in the wilderness, Prepare ye the way of the Lord, make his paths straight.

For the Hebrews, this little tidbit didn't offer a lot of clarity, especially when hundreds of years passed from the time Isaiah said it and the arrival of Mary and Joseph to the stage. So before we continue with the Nativity story, we need to back up a few months and explain what was going on in Judea.

The Priesthood

Before I talk about Zacharias (also known as Zechariah, etc.), let's review what was happening with organized religion. Way back in the time of Moses, Aaron was given the title of High Priest and the Tribe of Levi was established as the official pool for future high priests. All of these really fun laws were established around fourteen centuries before Jesus, but there was also a lot of upheaval in those fourteen centuries.

Want a frame of reference?

Think about how the role and definition of Pope changed in fourteen centuries of European history. Babylonians disrupted tradition. Assyrians disrupted tradition. Greeks disrupted tradition. Romans disrupted tradition.

For two centuries prior to Christ, the role of High Priest had become a hereditary and politically appointed position in order to "control the masses" in Judea. It is difficult for me to ascertain how "holy" any of these appointees were, but my gut instinct is that most reverent Jews probably respected the office but probably doubted the man.

A Certain Priest

While there was a public leader, it makes me wonder if they had private spiritual leaders. Could Zacharias have been one of those spiritual leaders?

[Luke 1:5] There was in the days of Herod, the king of Judaea, a certain priest named Zacharias, of the course of Abia: and his wife was of the daughters of Aaron, and her name was Elisabeth. [7] And they had no child, because that Elisabeth was barren, and they both were now well stricken in years.

Surprisingly, there is quite a bit going on in this little introduction. First, we learn that Zacharias is not just a minor priest in some obscure Judean village but a priest of the "order of Abia (Abijah)."

The order of what?

Well, this goes way back to the beginnings of the priesthood. Twenty-four Levites were chosen to take a turn with "voluntary church service." Abia (Abijah) was the 8th of 24. From what I could gather, this meant he would serve for two weeks during the year. Now, I'm not sure if they served two weeks in a row or twice a year.

Another interesting tidbit is the "daughters of Aaron" title given to Elizabeth. Without even knowing what this meant, it appears as if she is special, or why else would Luke bring this up. Remember, marriage was supposed to happen within a tribe. So Levites were supposed to marry Levites, but Elizabeth was REALLY special because she was of the "order of Aaron," which made her a super-Levite. I bring this up now because Mary is related to Elizabeth. Does this mean Jesus also has Levite blood?

So Zacharias must have been extra special to marry a woman with such a pedigree, right? Either his bloodline or righteousness must have warranted such quality marriage. Yes, he also could have been rich (but I'm not seeing it). Years later, Luke picks up on this important bit of research and includes it when introducing John the Baptist. Luke uses this to not only strengthen the case of John but with Mary (perhaps a daughter of Aaron also). If this theory is true, then Joseph would have been paying quite a "dowry" for a marriage to Mary.

[Luke 1:8] And it came to pass, that while he executed the priest's office before God in the order of his course, [9] According to the custom of the priest's office, his lot was to burn incense when he went into the temple of the Lord.

WHOA!

Time out.

Did Luke mean to say that Zacharias went into THE temple of the Lord? The TEMPLE OF THE LORD in Jerusalem? Solomon's Temple? The newly rebuilt Herod temple? I could dial this dramatic point back right now by saying no. He could just be serving in some Podunk village somewhere in some Podunk temple. Small potato priest in an unimportant town?

But what about all the buildup about Zacharias and Elizabeth in the paragraphs prior to this?

Yes, it does appear that we are talking about THE TEMPLE in Jerusalem. This will be supported later when it talks about Zacharias leaving and going home. If you preside in the town you live, this line doesn't make sense. If you live elsewhere and then have to travel to THE TEMPLE in Jerusalem, these lines work.

So let's explore the implications.

First, what are the rules about the temple? The only time the High Priest entered the inner sanctum of the "Holy of Holies" was on the Feast of Tabernacles (Also Day of Atonement and later Yom Kippur). This late summer feast (our September) was presided over by the HIGH PRIEST (which Zacharias was certainly not). Something is not right.

Well, it only says incense and the full ceremony involved sprinkling of blood, so this whole theory could be dismissed with that omission.

However, since the days of Aaron, a lot had changed. The Ark of the Covenant is gone, the old Solomon Temple was destroyed, and the High Priest office was hijacked by the Romans and Herod. What if this was the "unofficial" ceremony? Back in the day, the High Priest wore a rope around his neck in case he was unworthy and would be killed for profaning the inner sanctum. If the office was corrupt (see Caiaphas), then either it was still dangerous or the ceremony was avoided. Or…the legit priests drew lots to see who would do it in lieu of an actual religious leader.

I think this might be what is happening. If this were just a daily "incense" burning, why would there be a crowd? A legit Levite with a legit wife is drawn by lots because he is deemed worthy by the people (who are waiting reverently outside). The "Official" high priest is not allowed to do this. There are all sorts of ways to pop a hole in this theory, but bear with me, because I think it is important for John to be conceived in September during the Feast of Tabernacles.

This distinction might seem boring, but it will matter later when we determine birthdays for John and Jesus.

[Luke 1:10] And the whole multitude of the people were praying without at the time of incense. [11] and there appeared unto him an angel of the Lord standing at the right side of the altar of incense. [12] When Zacharias saw him, he was troubled and fear fell upon him.

Remember that there had been prophetic "silence" for the past few hundred years in ole Israel since prophets like Malachi and Haggai gave their final remarks. Yes, the Maccabees had a few miracles, but an actual angelic messenger from God had not happened for a long time.

And who shows up?

None other than Gabriel himself (he makes it clear in 1:19).

There are two curious bits in these three verses (aside from the fact that an angel just showed up). First, I ponder the clarity of the verse describing Gabriel standing beside the "right side" of the altar. Is this the "right hand of the right hand" visual? Is Jesus supposed to represent the sacrificial altar, and thus, Gabriel is his "right hand" guy? If so, this is quite an "Easter egg" (the kids use this phrase to mean clue/symbol) spoiler about things to come. The other bit I loved about this verse is the "fear" from Zacharias.

Option A (which is still cool): Zacharias is just a regular dude at a regular synagogue with a cheap, locally made altar and he is burning some regular incense in an unsanctified building with a bunch of bored locals outside waiting for him so they can go do some regular stuff. In this scenario, regular Zacharias is

SHOCKED because of the illustrious nature of his irregular guest. Dang, it's GABRIEL!

Option B (my preferred): Zacharias is 1 of 24 divisional priests who have superseded the duties of the Roman appointed High Priest and he drew lots/straws to determine who would go into the Holies of Holies in the LEGIT Temple in Jerusalem. Why draw? Remember, if you are not righteous, according to the old stories in the OT, you will drop dead! This is almost like Russian Roulette (I prefer to think of Indiana Jones 3). Zacharias draws the shortest straw for the Feast of Tabernacles. That would be scary. So if he does go in with the incense (and omitted blood), in the back of his mind, he might be worried about being worthy (and thus dropping dead). All is going well for him as he enters the main chamber and then the inner chamber (the Holiest of Holies). He is going about his duty when (DRAMATIC LIGHTING EFFECT) Gabriel shows up. Poor Zacharias probably thought he was about to die.

Even if Option B were wrong, seeing an actual ARCHANGEL would have been totally terrifying. Do a bit of Angel research, and you will see that they have an "appearance meter" where they can dial it down and almost be invisible, have it on low, where they appear like a regular human, or they can crank it up and appear so strange that they almost seem monstrous (see Daniel, Revelation, or Ezekiel for those multi-headed sightings). If you go with a medium to high "proof of authenticity" level, then I really feel for Zacharias.

> **[Luke 1:13] But the angel said unto him, Fear not, Zacharias: for thy prayer is heard; and thy wife Elisabeth shall bear thee a son, and thou shalt call his name John. [14] And thou shalt have joy and gladness; and many shall rejoice at his birth. [15]**

For he shall be great in the sight of the Lord, and shall drink neither wine nor strong drink; and he shall be filled with the Holy Ghost, even from his mother's womb."

The name John (in its shortened form) means "Jehovah's (pardon) gracious gift," which is obviously cool in all sorts of ways. But I'd like to put a twist on this a bit and preview the Elijah=John paradox that we'll be stepping into in a bit. Even though there is prophecy involving the return of Elijah, the official company line is that John is just John until after he is dead. Pay no attention to the man behind the curtain, kids. Everything is as it seems. He's just John. Could it be that Gabriel knew Zacharias and Elizabeth would put two and two together, and when trying to come up with a proper name, might have "jumped the shark" (another phrase the kids use to mean skipped to the end) and declared he is Elijah returned!

We'll put that odd thought on the back burner for a bit.

Now, the passage as a whole is obviously miraculous and hearkens back to the story of Abraham and Sarah. That seems to be the OBVIOUS meaning of "thy prayer is heard."

Really, Zacharias?

You're living in Roman-occupied Judea where torment and sin is running rampant and you pray for a child? You're the people's high priest. It's an important religious holiday. And you are thinking about yourself? Possibly…and whether you see this as sweet or selfish, it is the obvious human request for a couple that do not have a child. After all, Luke emphasized this among the few details we were given.

HOWEVER…just because a child is the result of his prayer, this does not absolutely mean this is what he prayed for. If you want to pick Zacharias as the #1 worthy, righteous choice to represent the Jews in the temple for the Feast of Tabernacles, then perhaps he DOES represent the people. And what do the people need? Christ! How do you get the Christ to come? Well, first Elijah must come back.

Filled with the Holy Ghost

Is this what he prayed for? Elijah? That would be unselfish and could also fit with what Gabriel said to him:

[Luke 1:13] But the angel said unto him, Fear not, Zacharias: for thy prayer is heard; and thy wife Elisabeth shall bear thee a son, and thou shalt call his name John. [14]And thou shalt have joy and gladness; and many shall rejoice at his birth. [15] For he shall be great in the sight of the Lord, and shall drink neither wine nor strong drink; and he shall be filled with the Holy Ghost, even from his mother's womb."

Verses fourteen and fifteen seem to anticipate the popularity of John the Baptist. In the next chapter, I'll get into more detail, but compared to Jesus, John was pretty cool and popular with the Jews? Why? He was bold, aggressive, and ready to talk smack about the ruling elite. He was perfect for a rebellion. Remember, this is what the Jews expected in a Messiah.

John is the G.O.A.T. (and I'm not talking about Azazel or scapegoats). John is the Greatest of All Time. He's going to be pretty awesome by human standards. (See Matt 11:11, now that is a resume builder).

The rest of John's preview involves a lifestyle that matches legends like Samson and the Nazirite. He's gunna be hard-core!

But lost in that preview is a very curious phrase "filled with the Holy Ghost, even from his mother's womb." WHAT?

In lesson six, you'll see how weird I really think JB is, but let's pry this apart now. First of all, the Holy Ghost arrives in force three decades from this point AFTER John is dead and AFTER Jesus dies on the cross. Even the disciples on the road to Emmaus were spiritually blind to scripture. The Holy Ghost arrives after Pentecost.

But not for JB!

Not only is he LIT with the Holy Ghost, but it is also from the womb. What does this mean in regards to Original Sin? You know, the thing that has plagued EVERY human since Adam and Eve. This Holy Ghost baby detail is vague and not clearly explained, but it leaves me with no other choice than to think: JOHN IS A WEIRD BABY. There will be a lot more on how weird in the next chapter, but this chapter belongs to Pa, so I should keep going.

> **[Luke1:16] And many of the children of Israel shall he turn to the Lord their God. [17]And he shall go before him in the spirit and power of Elias** (Elijah in other translations)**, to turn the hearts of the fathers to the children, and the disobedient to the wisdom of the just; to make ready a people prepared for the Lord.**

Okay, that's a weird baby indeed. See what Gabriel just did there? Zacharias sure saw it. After all, for the Christ to arrive, they all knew that Elijah would return from his flaming chariot ride to Heaven. Gabriel just said, "Yeah, <u>this</u> is that Malachi prophecy, Zach. Get ready! You're gonna have one weird baby."

Yes, it is weird that these two old folks are going to have a baby, but weirder still is that this baby is going to be filled with the Holy Ghost from the womb AND have something to do with the Elijah prophecy. Talk about your double whammies! It's no wonder Zacharias doesn't handle it well.

[Luke 1:18] And Zacharias said unto the angel, Whereby shall I know this? for I am an old man, and my wife well stricken in years.

Translation: Ha, ha, that's funny. I'm far too old for this to be true. Ha, ha, you must be joking.

Oh, Zacharias, don't back talk an angel.

[Luke 1:19] And the angel answering said unto him, I am Gabriel, that stand in the presence of God; and am sent to speak unto thee, and to shew thee these glad tidings. [20] And, behold, thou shalt be dumb, and not able to speak, until the day that these things shall be performed, because thou believest not my words, which shall be fulfilled in their season.

Translation: You talking to me? You talking to me? You must be talking to me, I'm the only one here (pardon the movie reference).

Yes, Gabriel is a bit insulted and reminds Zacharias (and the reader) about whom he happens to be. Now whether you ascribe to Billy Graham's angel list or the old school Thomas Aquinas list, humans have all sorts of views on angels. Both camps that I referenced believe there are Archangels and that Gabriel is one of the seven. However, there is (or was) a belief that sending an angel to earth (where there is sin) somehow taints that angel.

Yet Gabriel clearly refutes this "earthly" angel concept when he says he stands in front of the presence of God. Do you know what this means? (Think Moses). Yes, Hebrews, to stand in the presence of God, you must be blameless and pure. Gabriel brings up this detail to strengthen his case that I DON'T MAKE MISTAKES!

Hitting the Mute Button

I'm not sure if Gabriel mutes Zacharias or if this is God's decision, but the reason for it probably goes beyond back talk. Look at the next two verses first:

[Luke 1:21] And the people waited for Zacharias, and marveled that he tarried so long in the temple. [22] And when he came out, he could not speak unto them: and they perceived that he had seen a vision in the temple: for he beckoned unto them, and remained speechless.

Again, there is some flexibility of what "temple" you want your movie to be filmed at. Either way, there was a crowd outside (a big crowd if we're talking Jerusalem). Remember if this is the Feast of Tabernacles, they are worried he might not have been worthy and died during the ceremony. If there was any divine angel light (you've all seen the Christmas cards), then they are even more curious. Either way, if Zacharias had NOT been muted, what would he have done?

"Holy Cow (probably a bad interjection choice) I just saw Gabriel, and he told me my wife is going to help bring Elijah back via some weird baby! Oh, and the Christ is coming!"

This would have played out one of two ways. Version A—the Hannah Barbara Noah Version: Are you crazy, old man? What nonsense. He needs to retire! Get him out of the rotation. Ha, ha, ha! What a nut. (like that).

Version B—a Fuse is Lit. In this more likely version, the devout Jews (probably NOT the Roman-appointed guys like Annas or Caiaphas either) outside of the Temple would have gobbled this stuff up. It would have started a celebratory parade that would have been perceived as a riot or threat by the Romans, who would have cracked down, and death, death, and more death.

In Gabriel's version, Zacharias keeps his mouth shut and avoids the slaughter of Version B or the "easy-for-Herod-to-kill-you Version A. By muting Zacharias, they will all sense something weird has happened but will not lose their mind with zealous fanaticism.

> **[Luke 1:23] And it came to pass, that, as soon as the days of his ministration were accomplished, he departed to his own house. [24] And after those days his wife Elisabeth conceived, and hid herself five months, saying, [25] Thus hath the Lord dealt with me in the days wherein he looked on me, to take away my reproach among men."**

Even though there is not a lot of historical explanation on the "unofficial" Feast of Tabernacles ceremony, verse twenty-three supports the idea in my head. Zacharias went home. He was at a temple (somewhere) and went home (somewhere else). If this was all just a local ceremony and he was a local rabbi at a local synagogue, this travel detail does not make any sense. However, if he was living in say…Bethany…and he was 1 of 24 Kohen Priests, and HE was chosen to do the unofficial ceremony instead of the Roman-appointed guy, then traveling from Jerusalem (and the Temple) and back home would make a lot of sense.

"Hid." Team Jesus wants a low profile. See, that is how I saw Gabriel's mute button. In fact, this reminds me of how Jesus frequently told those who he cured to NOT tell anybody. They do not want mindless fanatics at this point. Both Elizabeth and Zacharias would share their good news with friends and family if it wasn't DANGEROUS.

It seems silly to hide for the first few months of a pregnancy, doesn't it? It seems more practical to hide during the last four months. I think part of this is that five months allowed everyone to settle down for a bit and forget it. After a few weeks of laying low, the curious friends outside of the Temple would have shrugged it off and gone about their lives. When she does "reveal" her pregnancy in the fifth month, there was no mention of Gabriel, Elijah, or Holy Ghost babies. Instead, she plays it pretty cool by saying, "Guess what, friends and neighbors?" Five months also pushes the calendar to the middle of winter.

Why does that matter?

If Zacharias served at the Feast of Tabernacles, this takes place in our modern September. Five months later would make it February. If she "revealed" her pregnancy in December, she would have had lots of Jewish guests during the Feast of Dedication. She and Zacharias kept it on the down low until all the religious pilgrims left Judea.

Meanwhile in Galilee…Gabriel visits Mary during the "sixth month" of Elizabeth's pregnancy, which pushes it to March. March is very close to the Passover Ceremony, which makes Mary's departure either very convenient or inconvenient. If it happens during the Passover, she could easily catch a ride. This also means the roads and highways could be full. Remember the

Trinity "overshadow" issue? Mary going to the "hill country" (either local hills or southern hills) seems to indicate a more difficult but more private trip. Was it a few weeks prior or a few weeks after? There are so many factors, huh?

But the BIG POINT is that it is around March. Do the math. March=our 3rd month. A pregnancy lasts nine months. 3+9=12. Holy Cow (I need a new phrase), that puts Jesus's birth at our December, doesn't it? We'll talk about Dec 25th later.

[Luke 1:39] And Mary arose in those days, and went into the hill country with haste, into a city of Juda (Judea); [40] And entered into the house of Zacharias, and saluted Elisabeth.

Again, the details of HOW she got there are really left to the imagination.

<u>Friends in Low Places</u>

We do learn that the HOUSE where Zacharias lives is definitely located in Judea (instead of Galilee). As long as you agree that Zacharias did not live in Jerusalem, then we're cool. Could he live in Emmaus? Sure. Hebron? Why not? Bethlehem? Slight problem. Bethany? Strong likelihood.

When we get to the chapter on the Magi, we'll discuss the problems with them living in Bethlehem, but for now, I'd like to focus on Bethany. Now there is nothing close to proof with this theory I have; it is simply conjecture. Decades after the Nativity, we learn that Jesus has a friend, Lazarus, in Bethany, which is a hike-over-the-mountain from Jerusalem. For a boy from Galilee, a trip to Jerusalem is kinda special. In fact, I would assume they'd only take the trip for the three religious holidays during the year. Based on historical records, we learn that Jerusalem during a festival swells beyond capacity. This would require you to have consistent housing. Think of it like a popular state park. If you are responsible, you book it a year in advance instead of just showing up. A devout family would make annual arrangements. See, this is why I think a kid from Nazareth became friends with a kid from Judea.

In other words, Mary and Joseph probably stayed at the same location every year, which is how Jesus became friends with Lazarus. We'll talk more about this later. The other thing about verse 40 is that she "entered the house" of Zacharias. If she were part of a convoy of pilgrims or her own family, folks in Bethany (or whatever town you want) would get excited. People would rush outside. There would be hugs and barking dogs (did Jesus have a puppy?) Yet if Mary traveled alone (which is what I think happened) she would have arrived in Bethany without fanfare and would have needed to walk inside to get their attention. If she was expected, these old folks would have kept an eye out for her, but nobody knew she was coming, especially alone. I think this is supported here.

Cue Elisabeth

[Luke 1:41] And it came to pass, that, when Elisabeth heard the salutation of Mary, the babe leaped in her womb;

Again, JB is an unnatural baby to recognize Mary and/or Jesus. Remember, Mary is NOT showing because she is only days into her pregnancy. We'll get into this full theory in the next chapter.

[Luke 1:41] and Elisabeth was filled with the Holy Ghost: [42] And she spake out with a loud voice, and said, Blessed art thou among women, and blessed is the fruit of thy womb. [43] And whence is this to me, that the mother of my Lord should come to me? [44] For, lo, as soon as the voice of thy salutation sounded in mine ears, the babe leaped in my womb for joy. [45] And blessed is she that believed: for there shall be a performance of those things which were told her from the Lord.**

The loud voice is strange. Was the Holy Ghost speaking through her? Was it simply excitement?

"Blessed art thou among women" is the best support for the Immaculate Conception theory, even though it is not clearly explained here. At worst, this is support that Mary was the golden ticket winner from a pool of every human woman since Eve. That's special enough, isn't it?

Next, I love the humility that Elizabeth immediately shows. Mary is a younger relative, who apparently has run away from home, and is in need of some serious questioning and chastising. Nothing about her arrival is natural or normal. No, Elizabeth's wise insight is a gift from the Holy Ghost (via her weird baby?) six months after her baby received the same gift. This allows her to not only get what is going on, but to also show her humility to the girl who should be treated as royalty. Think of the respect the current Queen of England gets. What the heck did she do? Nada. Mary? She was chosen to deliver the Christ (mic drop). Elizabeth also seems to understand that Mary has traveled some distance in order to reach the house (in Judea and possibly Bethany).

There is an insinuation that Mary has passed some sort of test by traveling (alone) to Elizabeth. Mary trusted Gabriel about the pregnancy and then trusted God that he would protect (and overshadow) her on the daring trip.

There is ZERO doubt happening here. There are no questions about the baby-daddy or her parents or what happened along the way. None of that. Instead, Elizabeth immediately recognizes that there is something AMAZING going on here. Remember, she did not witness Gabriel nor has Zacharias said a word. How does Elizabeth know what's going on? Was there more said than is written down. I guess the Holy Ghost detail means she was given details that should not have been obvious.

Mute Zacharias showed up in this scene also, but before I jump into the profound words spoken by Mary (chapter seven), let's get off track a bit and talk about the strange baby who is also part of this scene.

CHAPTER SIX

PREPARING THE WAY

Perhaps one of the biggest influences in our modern perceptions of Christmas is the annual Holiday Greetings card our friends and neighbors send us each December. In those cards, we see artistic depictions of Mary and Joseph, Angels, Shepherds, Wise Men, and various types of farm animals that may or may not have been found in Israel. If not Christmas cards, then surely the ceramic (or plastic) portrayals of these figures in Nativity scenes have locked things in mentally for us.

The expanded scene might even include art involving Zacharias and Elizabeth, who are captured with various poses of freak-out (cuz who wouldn't be losing it when Mary shows up with the Christ). But I can almost guarantee you've never picture a wee John the Baptist in this nativity story, have you? Yet there he was in the previous chapter thumping Elizabeth's womb as if to trumpet in the arrival of royalty. And when Jesus is born in

Bethlehem? Wee John is somewhere nearby in Judea with an "I told you so" look to all the other infants in the nursery.

If John had awareness of the Christ prior to even being born, then why did it take him thirty years to finally declare, "Behold…" at the River Jordan? It would be easy to just skip right over Wee John and jump into the Mary and Joseph story, but both the written innuendo and the unwritten "missing scenes" about this important figure are just too fun for me to skip over.

First, let's recap that MASSIVE bit of prophecy Gabriel dropped on Zacharias:

[Luke 1:16] And many of the children of Israel shall he turn to the Lord their God. [17] And he shall go before him in the spirit and power of Elias (Elijah in other translations)**, to turn the hearts of the fathers to the children, and the disobedient to the wisdom of the just; to make ready a people prepared for the Lord.**

Wee John is gonna be THE MAN! That is the easiest way to diminish this verse, by saying Gabriel is speaking metaphorically. E=Awesome. J=Awesome. E=J. Awesome=Awesome. In context of the Christmas story, this verse can easily get lost.

Even in context of the baptism story, John the Baptist can come off as an eccentric, loud prophet. But after he dies, Jesus drops some VERY heavy algebraic equations to make his disciples and the readers re-think everything they knew about John.

John is Elijah.

Huh?

We've had the luxury of 2,000 years of Biblical scholarship and this strange point still is as confusing as the day Jesus dropped it on his disciples, and before that, when Gabriel dropped it on Zacharias. If you are like me, you still insist on there being rules for a world where God spoke the world into existence with words and can cause miracles to happen whenever He wants to dispense with his laws of physics.

Christianity 101

Rules.

So before we take a leap of faith into J=E, let's make sure we can agree on some basics.

The penalty of sin is death, right?

Adam and Eve brought sin into the world? Genesis 101.

Adam and Eve (eventually) died because they sinned. Yup.

All human beings that sin also bear the penalty of death? Okay.

In the OT, Satan made sure all humans fell short in the eyes of

God? (See the Book of Job)

Jesus had to come to earth as a mortal human.

Jesus did not sin, and dying without sin, atoned for our sin.

These are some basic philosophies found in the Bible. Since Genesis, humans have died as a penalty for sinning. It's been a hard and fast rule since Adam and Eve…except for two people in the Old Testament…Enoch and Elijah. The Bible is fairly clear that these men did not experience death but were taken to heaven. Even though human pride would lead us to believe we know a lot about what it means to go to Heaven, none of us have a clue. Even enlightened men like Paul mentioned there being different parts to heaven. Thus it is difficult to even understand what it means for Enoch and Elijah to be taken to Heaven while still alive.

Is there some special room just for the two of them?

Are they in some sort of sub-heaven where they can exist while alive? Are they in the presence of God?

Can a living human even exist in the presence of God?

Are they in the presence of the souls of the dead?

Were there even human souls in Heaven (vs. Sheol) prior to Jesus living and dying on earth?

Is this fair?

No…?

God was very clear that the penalty of sin is death. If Enoch or Elijah had managed to live a sinless life, then what is the need for Christ? NO HUMAN BEING BESIDES CHRIST HAS BEEN SINLESS (immaculate?)! Despite being righteous men, far better than any of us, these two men still had to have sinned. God did not take these men from earth because they were sinless. God did not spare these men death because he loved them more than he loves us. These men might have been taken to Heaven, but it does not mean God spared them death (he just postponed their death dates). All sinners owe God a death. Enoch and Elijah were not perfect…but God did have a plan for them. They were special, but not so special that they were above death.

DISCLAIMER: At this point I will shamelessly pitch a sequel I have in the works: ***Examining the End Times***. I cannot get into my Enoch theories here or I'll never get back to the Prayer of Mary (which is really cool).

Examining Elijah

Unlike Enoch, there are many stories about Elijah. By looking only at the Old Testament, it would be pretty easy to match Elijah with Enoch as the second witness in the Book of Revelation (Spoiler: Enoch=yes, Elijah=no). In Revelation 11:5, it tells that the two witnesses will be able to send fire from their mouth to consume anyone trying to harm them. In 1 Kings 18:38, Elijah called the fires of God to defeat his enemies. In fact, there are not many prophets that can rival the power of this mighty man. Let's review Elijah's feats:

1 Kings 17:1-8 Elijah proclaims a drought

1 Kings 17:8-16 Miraculous replenishing of food

1 Kings 17:17-24 Elijah asks God to restore life to a boy.

1 Kings 18 Elijah slaughters the priests of Baal

1 Kings 19 Elijah eats a cake made by the Angel of the Lord

1 Kings 19 Elijah visits Mt. Horeb (Sinai) and stays in the same cave as Moses.

1 Kings 20-22 Elijah warns the wicked

2 Kings 2 Elijah ascends to Heaven

2 Kings 2 Elisha continues the fight.

2 Kings 13 Elisha dies.

Obviously, Elijah was a powerful man of God. He also was a killer. He killed men. Even though they were evil men, he still sinned and owes God a death. But what a candidate for the second witness! (I certainly could be wrong about eliminating him from the list).

Perhaps the most convincing factor in being a witness is his sojourn to Mt. Horeb in chapter 19. Elijah did not view himself as perfect, and even asks for his death for being no better than his fathers. Then he has a visitor. Some think that the Angel of the Lord is not just an ordinary angel but the preincarnate Christ. Now that really qualifies him as a witness. He's been chosen by Christ himself. At this meeting with the Angel of the Lord, he is given cake. This angel cake sustained him on a walk to Mt. Horeb, which is also known as Mt. Sinai. This is the same mountain where Moses met with God and received the 10 commandments. Whether Mt. Horeb is Mt. Jabal Musa or Jabal al Lawz, it is still a long walk without food or water for 40 days. This was a special food. In fact, I believe it could be manna. With manna/cake in his belly, Elijah was easily sustained on this walk.

Once he got to Mt. Horeb, he entered the sacred cave of God where he conversed with the Almighty. In God's direct hotline, Elijah wrapped his mantle around his body to protect him from God's holy presence.

Much later, Elijah took his apprentice Elisha with him to witness his ascension to Heaven. A chariot of fire came down and took Elijah up into Heaven. Elisha saw all of this and told others. In fact, Elijah made such a lasting impact on the Jewish people, that many years later, the prophet Malachi made a prophecy concerning the prophet.

[Malachi 4:5] Behold, I will send you Elijah the prophet before the coming of the great and dreadful day of the LORD: [6] And he shall turn the heart of the fathers to the children, and the heart of the children to their fathers, lest I come and smite the earth with a curse.

Elijah wasn't going to just stay in Heaven…he was coming back. Now, many End Times experts take the easy path and say all this adds up to make Elijah the 2nd witness.

This verse from Malachi almost seals the deal…almost.

To us, the great and dreadful day of the Lord sounds like Revelation. To Malachi, this also could have meant the coming of Christ as a Man. But Jesus didn't want to smite the earth, right? He came to save it. However, think of the lesson of the fig tree during Easter Week (Mark 11:12-26). Fig Tree<Jerusalem<Judea<the whole world. If there weren't people worthy of dying for, Jesus could have cursed the entire world just as easily as he cursed the fig tree. (Fate and Free Will makes my head hurt).

The Elijah Mission: A JLW Paraphrase.

God saw a pretty intense servant in Elijah, and without the suspension of any rules (which He has authority to suspend if He wanted), he chose to suspend the death of Elijah by sending down a flaming chariot to bring him to Heaven. The purpose of "suspending" the death sentence is for him to spend a few centuries in Heaven reading the LET'S SAVE HUMANITY PLAYBOOK, and right before Jesus would come to earth, Elijah would be sent back down to earth to provide an intense training session so that at least one person (remember Noah) would be worthy and ready to receive direct training from Jesus.

Isn't that what Malachi promised?

Just like all of the Christ prophecies were not exactly how the Pharisees imagined, so too was the Elijah prophecy much stranger than even Zacharias might have imagined. I'm sure Zacharias expected the window of Heaven to open back up, and then for the flaming chariot to do a Maverick-like flyby (Top Gun reference, sorry) of the Temple of Jerusalem while shouting out pithy phrases worthy of Santa Claus.

Instead, Gabriel told him Elijah was coming back in Wee John.

That's impossible! (said the Hebrews after each and every absurdly powerful miracle they witnessed).

Okay, okay, I'll try to give you some precedent (and rules).

A Double Portion

Check out <u>2 Kings 2:9</u>. In this verse, Elisha asks for a "double portion" of Elijah's spirit.

What?

Elisha knew his mentor was leaving. Elisha would now be the lead man in the fight against evil. He probably worried he didn't have enough power to sustain the cause. But rather than simply asking for his own strength as Joshua had after Moses left, Elisha asked for Elijah's spirit.

What does that mean?

We do not even understand how our own soul works, so we definitely do not understand how Elijah's powerful soul worked.

But the request is granted. Elisha isn't even sure if it is possible or if it'll work. But as soon as Elijah goes to Heaven, something does happen. He gets a part of Elijah's spirit. It would be easier to just think that Elisha was given more power by the Holy Spirit or God, but that is not how this scene is described. From that moment the mantle fell on him, Elisha was more than he once was.

Perhaps the easiest way to understand this could be from a classic piece of pop culture. Just as Obi Wan Kenobi guided Luke Skywalker in spirit, perhaps part of Elijah's soul guided Elisha. Or perhaps it is even more explicit than that. What if Elijah could divide his soul? Perhaps part of his soul continued to exist with his physical body in Heaven while the other part of his soul stayed with Elisha.

Isn't that what this scene describes? Who are we to know what God can or can't do? Even Elijah wasn't sure this could happen, but it seems that it did.

Now, from this moment, Elisha really started to act just like Elijah too. He divided the river Jordan just as he'd done earlier. He healed, he struck wicked youths dead out of anger, he raised a child from death.

Now I do not believe Elijah possessed Elisha and took him over, but what if two spirits could inhabit a human body. It works for demons, why not for the good guys?

When Elisha dies in Chapter 13, things are still not normal. When a dead man incidentally touched the bones of Elisha, he was brought back to life. One thing is clear...Elisha died. So what happened to the spirit of Elijah? The rest of his spirit was in Heaven still with his body. Did he half die? Can such a thing be so?

One thing is undisputable...Elijah was expected back. Malachi knew this. But how? No one had ever come back before. Enoch hadn't. What was going to happen to Elijah? The Jews probably expected thunder bolts and lightning (very, very frightening) and earthquakes when Elijah returned.

Cuz Jesus Said So

According to Jesus, everyone missed it.

How did we miss that? It doesn't say anything about Elijah in the New Testament, does it?

Ah, we're right back in the Christmas story, aren't we?

Let's get this straight. According to Gabriel, Wee John will have a direct connection to the verse from Malachi. Wee John will fulfill Malachi. Could it be that the child will be given the 2nd half of Elijah just like Elisha had been given the first half?

As far as the Christmas story goes, Wee John vanishes from reference and imagination right after that womb kick he gave Elizabeth, but Wee John grew up to be John the Baptist.

In this manner, he definitely fulfilled the prophecy of preparing the way for Christ. Unlike Christ, the Jews warmly embraced the preaching of John and quickly embraced him as a prophet of God.

While we do not have any stories of his childhood, we do know that he shared many similarities with Elijah that did not go unnoticed by the leaders of the church.

He dressed in animal skins like Elijah
He ate locust and honey like Elijah
He inspired fear and awe like Elijah
He openly condemned the king of Judea like Elijah
He knew he'd been sent to prepare the way for Christ.

If I was a lawyer, I might have declared "I have no further questions, Your Honor, and then sat down with a wry look to the other attorney. But then the other attorney (the Pharisees) destroy my entire case with John 1:19:

> **[John 1:19] And this is the record of John, when the Jews sent priests and Levites from Jerusalem to ask him, Who art thou? [20] And he confessed, and denied not; but confessed, I am not the Christ. [21] And they asked him, What then? Art thou Elias** (Elijah)**? And he saith, I am not. Art thou that prophet? And he answered, No."**

I guess that wraps it up. John denied it. He said he is not Elijah. Unfortunately, John probably had some very good reason for saying this. What if he had said he *was* Elijah? The country would have exploded with faux-religious fervor. No one would have listened to his preparation. John's mission was to prepare the way. Answering *"Yes"* would have undone his message.

However, even though he says no twice, look what he says a few verses later:

> **[John 1:22] Then said they unto him, Who art thou? that we may give an answer to them that sent us. What sayest thou of thyself? [23] He said, I am the voice of one crying in the wilderness, Make straight the way of the Lord, as said the prophet Esaias** (Isaiah).

What kind of answer is that? No, NO, Yes.

Okay, who blew up the Death Star in Star Wars? Luke Skywalker.

Or was it Obi Wan Kenobi?

Luke pushed the trigger, but if not for Obi Wan Kenobi being there every step of the way and convincing Luke to trust the Force, Luke would have failed.

So John's answer is: I'm John, *and* I'm the Elijah prophecy. I'm John the Elijah.

If you are unconvinced, so too were the Pharisees, who thought they had their man. Later, it was Jesus that explained things better.

Preaching in the Wilderness

Before we get to that, let's back up to John the Baptist's second interaction with Jesus the Christ. Aside from the womb kick, I do not know if John the Elijah saw Jesus again for another thirty years.

All four Gospel writers take time to give "John the Elijah" a proper introduction. We learn he is the son of Zacharias, but we already knew that. Oh, and his style, yep, we already knew that. There is a line that I find curious—John preached in the wilderness.

The quickest assumption is to call the River Jordan "the wilderness" because that is where we see him when he baptizes Jesus. Geographically, this is the heart of old Israel. Heck, Galilee is more of a distant wilderness than the Jordan River. The Jordan River is about twenty miles from Jerusalem, a city where a million people can gather during a given festival. This is not "wilderness" even if it is rocky.

Do you know what the wilderness could be? The Arabian desert between Judea and Parthia (Iraq). Now that is a wilderness!

With this logic, I could argue the Gobi Desert is the wilderness too, but let me turn a corner to why I think it is important.

Did the Jews once live in Babylon for a generation or two?

Where do the Magi see the "star"?

Where do scholars think Magi are from?

Yes, I think there is some loose support for there being a devout fan base of all things Christ related in Parthia (Babylon), but after the dispersion, there are Jewish communities in a lot of places besides Judea, right?

That could be important.

Tough Times to be an Infant

We're going to go back to the Christmas story for a bit, but preview the events of later chapters, involving Herod (cue the Darth Vader Imperial March theme).

Even though we don't hear anything from John the Baptist again, he had to have been a six-month-old baby when Jesus was born in Bethlehem. He was also a seven-month-old baby when Jesus was brought to the Temple to be passed around by some really old people. And when the Wise Men showed up? He must have been around during that time also.

At some point, Herod LOSES it and decides the only course of action is to kill EVERY baby in Bethlehem, Think about the evil willpower to do something like that. If he is willing to kill every baby in Bethlehem, would there be any baby from a newborn to the age of two that would be safe?

Wee John is in grave danger!

Later, we will discuss the "house" where Mary and Joseph stay prior to bringing Jesus to the temple. This "house" is probably where they are staying when the Magi show up unexpectedly. Regardless of whose "house" this happens to be, Wee John is also in a house very close to the one Jesus was staying at.

If Herod kills the Christ, he wins.

If Herod kills the Elijah (prior to his preparation), he also wins.

Okay, so maybe Herod doesn't have this on his radar. Maybe all the other 24 Kohanim priests can keep a secret about Wee John and Mute Zacharias (doubtful but possible). While Mary, Joseph, and Jesus are getting out of Dodge en route to Egypt, Zacharias and Elizabeth also have an important decision: is it safe to keep Wee John, aka John the Elijah, in Judea?

This is why I really like the idea of John growing up in distant Parthia. He had a ride (the Magi). He had an audience (the Babylonian Jews who stayed). He had a great academic learning center (Parthia). Plus, there is an entire legend from Mandaeism about John beginning his baptism ministry in Parthia (Iraq).

The Baptist Meets the Christ

There is also a practical reason to want John in a distant wilderness…it takes thirty years for him to meet Jesus.

Now remember, Jesus was buddies with Lazarus, a Judean from Bethany. This insinuates that during Jesus's approximate ninety trips to Judea during his life that he regularly met Lazarus.

Yet John the Baptist, who is a maternal biological relative of Jesus, doesn't once meet Jesus before the day he sees him approach the river to be baptized.

I think Luke 3:1 has the reason. John turns thirty. I've read a few articles that may or may not be credible that explained that at the age of thirty, Hebrew men were able to preach and teach and read in the synagogue (Bar Mitzvahs are a more recent custom). If John grew up and evangelized in Judea for thirty years, then why the sudden interest from the Pharisees? For the first ten years of his life, it would have been dangerous to be identified as the son of Zacharias and to be the same age as the Christ, even if Herod was dead. It would have been smart and safe for him to stay in Parthia. What would he have done in Parthia?

Evangelize 'til he was blue in the face! To both Jew and Gentile.

So by the time he reaches thirty, worldly travelers would have told stories about this Christ-aged young man who could rip scripture like he was a prophet. "John the Elijah" would have gained fame prior to returning to his home when he reaches the age of thirty. Just like when they were infants, "John the Elijah" has a six-month head start before Jesus shows up.

What does he do with this head start? The obvious answer is to say he called out the corruption in Judea. The best answer is that he took on two apprentices/disciples—Andrew the son of Jonah and John the son of Zebedee. What happened after he declared Jesus to be the Christ and baptized him? Having prepared the way, he handed over his prize pupils to become 2 of the 12 disciples that would spread Christianity to the entire world.

If this guy really did live his life in the style of Elijah, then it makes sense that he lasts less than a calendar year in Judea before being arrested.

The J=E Theory

Are you ready to get back to the J=E theory?

John the Baptist once again recognized the Christ just by being in close proximity. After all, the Elijah part spent the better part of five centuries with him in Heaven. So John the Baptist also knew that once Jesus knelt to be baptized, the mission was not over yet. If he was privy to the LET'S SAVE HUMANITY PLAYBOOK, then he knew Jesus had a bunch of prophecies to fulfill, which he asked about from his prison cell.

[Matthew 11:7] And as they departed, Jesus began to say unto the multitudes concerning John, What went ye out into the wilderness to see? A reed shaken with the wind? [8] But what went ye out for to see? A man clothed in soft raiment? behold, they that wear soft clothing are in kings' houses. [9] But what went ye out for to see? A prophet? yea, I say unto you, and more than a prophet. [10] For this is he, of whom it is written, Behold, I send my messenger before thy face, which shall prepare thy way before thee. [11] Verily I say unto you, Among them that are born of women there hath not risen a greater than John the Baptist: notwithstanding he that is least in the kingdom of heaven is greater than he. [12] And from the days of John the Baptist until now the kingdom of heaven suffereth violence, and the violent take it by force. [13] For all the prophets and the law prophesied until John. [14] And if ye will receive it, this is Elias (Elijah)**, which was for to come. [15] He that hath ears to hear, let him hear.**

J=E

Really?

There we have it. Jesus tried his best to spell it out for us. John is more than a prophet. He is the fulfillment of prophecy. He is Elijah. Who do we believe? John or Jesus. I'll go with Jesus. Jesus didn't expect people to get it. It is an abstract concept.

This isn't the only place we have a connection between John the Baptist and Elijah.

Double Portion, Double Death

Matthew 17 describes the transfiguration of Jesus on the mountain. Jesus took Peter, James and John (sons of Zebedee) to this high mountain. On the mountain, Moses and Elijah appeared to Jesus.

First, I'd like to remind everybody in this courtroom that Moses is officially dead.

What about Elijah? Coincidentally, John the Baptist had just been executed. If part of his soul had died with Elisha and part of his soul died with John the Baptist, it seems Elijah had given God his death (twice). That is why Elijah was now able to meet with Jesus. This wasn't John the Baptist because Jesus hardly knew the man. Jesus did know Elijah from Elijah's time in heaven. They both went down about the same time. They shared and understood the mission.

Heading into his darkest hour, Jesus needed advice and inspiration from both Moses and Elijah.

Seeing Elijah, the disciples wondered if the Malachi prophecy had been wrong. They knew the Son of God was Jesus. They also (somehow) recognized Elijah (did Jesus greet them? Name tags? Divine obviousness?). But they knew Elijah was supposed to return prior to the Messiah.

Well the Messiah had come and they hadn't seen Elijah return to earth in physical form. John and Elijah must not have looked alike.

Jesus explains this in:

[Matthew 17:10] And his disciples asked him, saying, Why then say the scribes that Elias (Elijah) **must first come? [11] And Jesus answered and said unto them, Elias** (Elijah) **truly shall**

first come, and restore all things. [12] But I say unto you, That Elias (Elijah) **is come already, and they knew him not, but have done unto him whatsoever they listed. Likewise shall also the Son of Man suffer of them. [13] Then the disciples understood that he spake unto them of John the Baptist.**

Elijah has come already?

He came as John the Baptist. No one understood. We can clearly see that John was Elijah when Jesus said that they did to Elijah whatever they wished. John the Baptist was beheaded by his own people. When on earth, Elijah was not killed by anyone. Jesus said he'd "likewise" suffer like Elijah suffered. Elijah had died with John the Baptist. Jesus knew John and Elijah were one and the same.

DISCLAIMER: I will continue to argue this point during a discussion of the "Two Witnesses of Revelation" in my future publication *Examining the the Beloved Disciple*. Spoiler (Moses=no, Elijah=no, Enoch=Yes. For witness #2, you'll have to buy the book when it comes out).

Now, where were we?

Ah, yes. Mary (barely a week pregnant) just walked all the way down from Nazareth and barged into the house of Zacharias, where she met Elizabeth (six months pregnant with a very unique baby).

CHAPTER SEVEN

SONGS AND BLESSINGS

So wherever you want Zacharias' house located (choose Bethany!), there is an amazing collection of spiritual heavyweights sitting around the kitchen table.

To quickly recap, back in September, Zacharias went in to the Temple, met Gabriel, and returned home where Elizabeth was pregnant with super-embryo, "John the Elijah." Six months later (near Passover in March), Mary also gets a visit from Gabriel and promptly bolted for Judea. In the last chapter, you saw how both Wee John and Elizabeth reacted with complete confidence that this was the fulfillment of the Christ prophecy.

All caught up?

Now I've seen a lot of Christmas movies where filmmakers try to capture the Virgin Mary on film. Most get the devout aspect right (solemn expression with knowing eyes), but they often try to "humanize" Mary for the audience by filling her with doubt, fear, uncertainty, etc. While these are certainly natural responses for mere believers like Zacharias or you and I, I've rarely seen filmmakers use Luke 1:46-55 because, let's face it, soliloquys went out of style four centuries ago. Mary's LONG greeting is extremely wordy where an empathetic hug and a few tearful laughter exchanges suffice for good actresses to convey the weight of this moment.

But the Song of Mary ROCKS!!!!

These heavy verses show that the young woman chosen by the Trinity is indeed a spiritual superhero with a profound understanding of the big picture.

[Luke 1:46]: And Mary said, 'My soul doth magnify the Lord,

[47] And my spirit hath rejoiced in God my Saviour.

[48] For He hath regarded the low estate of his handmaiden: for, behold, from henceforth all generations shall call me blessed.

[49] For He that is mighty hath done to me great things; and holy is his name.

[50] And His mercy is on them that fear Him from generation to generation.

[51] He hath shewed strength with His arm; He hath scattered the proud in the imagination of their hearts.

[52] He hath put down the mighty from their seats, and exalted them of low degree.

[53] He hath filled the hungry with good things; and the rich He hath sent empty away.

[54] He hath holpen his servant Israel, in remembrance of his mercy;

[55] As He spake to our fathers, to Abraham, and to His seed for ever."

Let's start with her humility. She just won the lottery. She had an "overshadowing" encounter with God, the Holy Spirit, the Christ, as well as Gabriel. She received more attention than any human since Adam and Eve. Mary would have spiritually floated from Nazareth to Judea. Can you imagine the "grace" high she would have felt? If I were Mary, when Elizabeth got done greeting me, I probably would have said something stupid like, "Yeah, I know! Cool, huh?"

The opening lines not only show her humility, but by the end of the open lines, she not only refers to her "low estate" but also that she is a "handmaiden." If you use an app like Biblehub, you can see that the English word varies from bondservant to servant girl, which all make the right point. She is a servant. She does not see herself as the Queen of Heaven and Earth but instead as a meek servant.

Which begs the question…how will she serve?

Obviously, she will serve by giving birth to Jesus, but she's also gonna be the world's greatest mother, right?

How Omni is Baby Jesus?

Hold on a second.

The Christmas story does not contain any explanation as to how to imagine the Christ child, but this is a HUGE concept to ponder. I don't mean to simplify things, but let's just examine the two ways to see things. Option A is that the Christ takes on human flesh in the form of baby Jesus but is born both Omniscient and Omnipotent. When we see Jesus later in the Gospels, he is fully capable of any miracle he wants (omnipotent) and also seems to know the past, present, and future (omniscient). He is truly God on earth.

But when did that start?

In the womb? Upon birth? Upon circumcision? During his terrible twos? At twelve? His teen years? Or when he reached thirty? Upon baptism in the Jordan River?

An O&O baby Jesus is very hard for me to comprehend. How do you let him leave your house in Nazareth? Why would this wunderkind even need parents? Or teachers?

Ah, that anecdote at age twelve does show a Jesus that amazes the teachers, right?

Yes, but if you back that up to age four, Jesus would be a bit terrifying to anybody he comes into contact with. It would have been seen as unnatural, right? This leaves us with an O&O baby Jesus who just fakes his own infancy and childhood until he can start letting his O&O out, or Jesus came to earth to be tested.

To be tested, you could not be hardwired to be infallible or it wouldn't be a test. I'm a teacher, and if I handed the kids all the answers to the test (being omniscient) and then wanted to test them, it would be a pretty lame test, right? What did it prove? Nothing. Would I be proud of any of my students for acing the test? No, they cheated. For it to be a test, there needs to be something on the line, right?

Wiring Jesus to be omniscient and omnipotent from birth would not prove much except that God could possess a body. I do not subscribe to the O&O theory from birth. For the record, I think the baptism of Jesus is the end of a test. From birth to age 30, he was tested daily, and by the time he walked down the shore of the Jordan, he'd passed every test life had thrown at

him. Hate, lust, lying, stealing, jealousy, and even parental diso-
bedience were certainly thrown at Jesus during these years,
right? So by the time we get to age thirty, Jesus has not only
been exposed to most sins but passed each test.

Then John the Baptist shouts out for all to come forward and
be baptized in order to wash away sin. A fully O&O Jesus would
have scoffed at this idea if he was all-knowing enough to know
he hadn't sinned yet. An O&O Jesus would have clicked the answer to the test and immediately have seen it light up green for
getting it right. By the time he got to question #1235 on the ex-
am, he would know with certainty that when he submitted the
test, he'd have a 100%.

My Jesus walked into the river.

This test was pride. The Jesus that walked into the Jordan did
not say to himself or those watching, "No need, I'm perfect."
Remember how Job would pound on his righteous chest and ask
to understand his sin? Pride is the same sin that got Satan. All of
his life, Jesus lived with people who **knew** he was the Christ, yet
he had the humility to still go into the water.

Remember the students with the cheat sheet? When God sees
Jesus walk into the water, God opens up a window of Heaven
and declares, "You are my beloved Son; in You I am well
pleased."

Translation: Congratulations, you aced the test.

I think God was pleased because there **was** something on the
line. From childhood to this penultimate moment, there were
countless tests that Jesus could have failed (but he didn't). Even
the final test of baptism was an illogical trap that he passed, and
the result was not only an acknowledgement from God that all

the rumors were true, but that is also when the Holy Spirit descended upon him. The purpose? From this moment, he walked around as an Omniscient and Omnipotent Jesus whose sole purpose was to set up a team of humans who would spread the Gospel to the world.

I think that Jesus was born without a restrictor plate and at any moment in those thirty years, he could have proven Satan right about humanity by sinning. Speaking of Satan, right after being Baptized (see John's account) Jesus brings his newest disciples back to Galilee where he meets his mother Mary, who leans over to him during the wedding at Cana and comments about the hosts running out of wine. And how does O&O Jesus respond?

[John 2:4] Jesus saith unto her, Woman, what have I to do with thee? Mine hour is not yet come. [5] His mother saith unto the servants, Whatsoever he saith unto you, do it.

Mom? Notice how Mary recognizes that the regular Jesus who might have listened to her frivolous comment about wine is different than the O&O Jesus sitting beside her. He'd passed the "pride" test and now was fully Omniscient and Omnipotent (but still needed to go see Satan in the wilderness and still fulfill the prophecies, which is the comment about his hour not coming yet). Mary recognized that this is no longer her son/student. She was looking into the eyes of her Lord and Savior, which is why Mary shifted gears and prepped the servants to do whatever he asked. Then the miracles began to happen, didn't they?

The Teacher of Eternity

I apologize for getting a bit off track, but I did bring it back around to Mary, so let's go back to the Song of Mary for a minute. My VERY long point is that Mary knows she is a servant.

Her job?

To teach Jesus.

To arm Jesus.

To guide Jesus.

Yes, Mary (and Joseph) are the greatest Sunday school teachers of all time. The Holy Spirit cheat sheet did not arrive until Jesus was 30, which meant (I believe) He went through his early life with only the tutelage of Mary and Joseph. At the River Jordan, Mary's star student passed the pride test, showed her his A+ report card at the wedding in Cana, and then went out to use the weapons she'd given him to be tempted by Satan, who had flunked <u>his</u> pride test. How did Jesus beat Satan? With Bible verses!

Teacher of Eternity Award!

This is why I love that Mary sees herself as a servant, and for the next thirty years (especially those early years), how could she let herself get distracted from her servitude?

[Luke 1:48] for, behold, from henceforth all generations shall call me blessed.

Mary totally understands how the Christ Plan is supposed to unfold. Remember how the disciples struggled with the concept that Jesus would die and that the End Times would NOT come until the Gospels were spread to all nations (which took a while). Mary seems to understand the length of the timeline, doesn't she? "All" generations could not only mean the last two thousand years, but perhaps even the previous four thousand years worth of Christ Plan believers (Adam and Eve were the first two members) who were waiting with King David in Sheol.

Even though the Book of Revelation will not be given for several decades, she also seems to have a basic understand of how that will go down:

[Luke 1:49] For he that is mighty hath done to me great things; and holy is his name.

Yes, this could be a God (YHWH) reference, and it could also be a reference to the name Jesus, but since the purpose of this book is to expand the box, take a look at the Book of Revelation

[19:11] And I saw heaven opened, and behold a white horse; and he that sat upon him was called Faithful and True, and in righteousness he doth judge and make war. [12] His eyes were as a flame of fire, and on his head were many crowns; and he had a name written, that no man knew, but he himself. [13] And he was clothed with a vesture dipped in blood: and his name is called The Word of God. [14] And the armies which were in heaven followed him upon white horses, clothed in fine linen, white and clean. [15] And out of his mouth goeth a sharp sword, that with it he should smite the nations: and he shall rule them with a rod of iron: and he treadeth the winepress of the fierceness and wrath of Almighty God. [16] And he hath on his vesture and on his thigh a name written, KING OF KINGS, AND LORD OF LORDS.

There is a ton of "holy name" reference in this epic prophecy about Jesus. If you truly are the T.O.E (Teacher of Eternity), it would be a shame to only use these talents and gifts once, right? Oh wait! Doesn't Jesus put Mary and John together while on the cross. Even though John the Disciple has a mother, the Beloved Disciple (who writes the Book of Revelation) gets placed with the Teacher of Eternity (who seemed to already get it).

[Luke 1:50] And his mercy is on them that fear him from generation to generation.

Again, I love the full scope Mary seems to understand here. Not only could you see this as a reference to us (the last 2000 years) but it also could be a reference to the entire Christ Plan believers like King David, Abraham, and Moses.

[Luke 1:51] He hath shewed strength with his arm; he hath scattered the proud in the imagination of their hearts.
[52] He hath put down the mighty from *their* seats, and exalted them of low degree.

Now, this is what I'm talking about. First of all, even if you want your Mary to be uneducated, this is some pretty gnarly language used here from a young peasant girl. To me, this is further proof that Mary is special. Remember the Daughters of Aaron "title" given to Elizabeth. Well, if Mary and Elizabeth are related, perhaps Mary just doesn't have good stock but might also be afforded a higher status for a future bride of a devout man. Did Mary get trained?

This passage is not accidental, and shows an understanding of Old Testament scripture. Her two verses referenced Isaiah 51 (Arm/Rahab/Serpent) Psalm 74 (strength/leviathan/serpents) and Isaiah 27 (strong/Leviathan/serpent)

Go ahead and look them up, but let me paraphrase. These Old Testament tales talked about God fighting a primordial serpent, and with the strength of his arm, defeated the serpents. The most lukewarm commentators will say this is just reference to the older Baal legends. I strongly believe these are flashbacks to the Fall of Lucifer, who Jesus does witness being thrown from Heaven back in the day. The "mighty" that Mary talks about are more than just Herod and Pilate talk. In old Hebrew, Gibbor was a word that meant "mighty men" but was used in places where Nephilim and Giants were described. This is some epic talk referencing the Fallen Angels and the War in Heaven (Rev 12).

Peasant girl? I think not.

This shows a high degree of understanding not only for his earthly mission but also for his "big picture" mission, which ends with him defeating Satan (the Red Dragon) and casting him into the Lake of Fire.

[Luke 1:53] He hath filled the hungry with good things; and the rich he hath sent empty away.

So during Christ's ministry, he certainly fulfilled this prophecy (loaves and fishes) as well as the symbolic spiritual food he filled us with; however, I also want to leave you with a stranger thought. What sustained Mary during her trip from Nazareth to Judea? She is the sparrow. She is the raven. Aside from that EPIC moment when she was "overshadowed" and the Christ was made flesh, she might have also witnessed other little miracles in recent days as God provided comfort and protection to his handmaiden.

[Luke 1:54] He hath holpen (helped) his servant Israel, in remembrance of his mercy;
[55] As he spake to our fathers, to Abraham, and to his seed for ever.

Again, our uneducated peasant girl shows a PHD level understanding of the scope of the Christ prophecy seeing the Babylon exile as a mercy as well as the promise given to Abram that came to fruition in her womb. The complexity of this song shows she not only gets it but is also versed in scripture.

Three Months of?

Now, the next verse really leaves me wanting more. In the first few moments of arrival, we get all sorts of epic understanding from Wee John to a prophetic Mary. Then the next three months in Judea are silent:

[Luke 1:56] And Mary abode with her about three months, and returned to her own house.

What happened during these three months?

Remember, Zacharias can't speak yet, so thoughts of a strategic planning session for the future of Christianity cannot even be discussed. Did Mary and Elizabeth converse? Did they keep Mary hidden during those three months? Did Mary's family know where she was? Who she was with?

Heading into my chapter on Joseph, I'd also like to point out that Mary returned to "her own house" instead of returning to Joseph's house because the arranged time for their marriage has not happened yet. Also remember that heading back home at three months pregnant would not be an obvious vision (no gasp required on the profile shot) for anyone to be concerned about.

Perhaps the toughest thing to understand is why does Mary stay for three months and then leave right before Elizabeth is going to give birth. Why not wait another month? Did she go back alone? Did Zacharias send loyal men to accompany her? Did she even let them know she was going?

It makes me sad not to know these details.

Instead of answering these details, Luke keeps focus on Judea to show the details of Zacharias and Elizabeth.

[Luke 1:57] When the time came for Elizabeth to have her child, she gave birth to a son. 58Her neighbors and relatives heard that the Lord had shown her great mercy, and they rejoiced with her.

It seems as if Elizabeth's secret pregnancy is known in her village (Bethany?) when it mentions "neighbors and relatives." Yes, it certainly would have caused a stir to have the old lady next door about to give birth. Even if they didn't know about the Gabriel visit, it would have been a bizarre situation with a worrisome outcome worthy of a small crowd. This all seems reasonable. The strange word in this passage is the mention of relatives. Remember, Elizabeth is a "Daughter of Aaron," which means she is a member of a pretty righteous club. Are there other Team Jesus folks already assembled? Or…are these relatives from her "Mary of Nazareth" side? Are they also related to Mary, and if so, do they know Mary's secret situation as well? Is Elizabeth from Nazareth or is Mary from Bethany? Just because we meet Mary in Nazareth doesn't mean her family has been there for generations. If anything, Elizabeth being surrounded by relatives supports a family still anchored in Judea.

Naming Rights

[Luke 1:59] On the eighth day, when they came to circumcise the child, they were going to name him after his father

Zechariah. [60] But his mother replied, "No! He shall be called John." [61] They said to her, "There is no one among your relatives who bears this name." [62] So they made signs to his father to inquire what he wanted to name the child.

First, I'd like to preview the circumcision ritual established here. We will see this same ritual mentioned for Jesus, which makes a long stay in a donkey den very problematic.

What a strange name! Remember, Gabriel came up with the name, speaking this order directly to Zacharias, which means he certainly found a way to relay the message to his wife, who seems to be dialed in to the whole Christ plan. Elizabeth recoils because it is NOT a popular/common name.

This "naming" issue brings up a couple points.

First, it establishes that John the Son of Zebedee (John the Disciple=JD) is much younger than John the Son of Zacharias (John the Baptist=JB). This just supports my notions that JD was the youngest of the 12 disciples.

Second, it seems to sever the idea that the wife of Zebedee was NOT a relative of Mary. Remember my "Sister-in-law" theory about Mary Clopas? Others argue that Jesus is a cousin of JD and James, which makes their "discovery" of him at the Baptism scene very problematic (if they've known him their whole lives). JB was the FIRST time a "Daughter of Aaron" named their child by this name. When JD is born (up to 15 years later), does Zebedee name him John in tribute to the wunder-kind from Judea? Is JB already famous? And what a coincidence that JD becomes the apprentice of the man he was named after, John the Baptist.

After Elizabeth forcefully tells them "No!" to naming him Zach Junior, they go and overrule her by speaking to Zacharias through "signs." Kind of a jerk move.

[Luke 1:63] And he asked for a writing table, and wrote, saying, His name is John. And they marveled all. [64] And his mouth was opened immediately, and his tongue loosed, and he spake, and praised God. [65] And fear came on all that dwelt round about them: and all these sayings were noised abroad throughout all the hill country of Judaea. [66] And all they that heard them laid them up in their hearts, saying, What manner of child shall this be! And the hand of the Lord was with him."

What Manner of Child?

Fear! What scared them? Zacharias is an old man with years of experience serving the public and speaking. While it was strange that he had been silent for nine months, it would have been startling to hear him begin to speak but not worthy of fear. So what scared them? The most obvious answer is the message that followed, but since my purpose is to help the reader imagine all the possibilities, let's look at a peculiar alternative idea—baby John.

If "John the Embryo" was able to recognize the Christ through two wombs and kick his mother on cue, AND he was not just a regular baby but one with the spirit of Elijah downloaded into him, then there is a chance that this baby could have been weird from the beginning. Normal human babies take months and years to learn first how to control their bodies and then how to speak the language, but if John was imbued with

Elijah-ness, he could have had a dramatic jumpstart on the learning process.

Look at verse 66. What manner of child is this? Now that is a strange thing to say. Lots of people have shown me newborns, and regardless of how wrinkled that Shar Pei baby might be, even someone with social awkwardness like me can find something cute about a newborn. What manner of child is this? Not cool, neighbors and relatives, not cool at all. But what did they see? How did they KNOW Wee JB was different?

The answer is **"the hand of the Lord was with him."** Good grief, now I'm beginning to believe my own strange theory. What did the "hand" look like? Remember, Jesus was thirty when the Holy Spirit descended upon him; Wee JB was born lit up. Even though the text does not say, they KNEW there was something strange about the baby.

Whether Zacharias's words or his strange baby, Wee JB does seem to serve a purpose: a strategic distraction. The Christ Plan was subtle, and the Jews wanted grandiose. Any sort of sign or omen would fuel up their hope, which is why these neighbors and friends began spreading the stories in Judea and abroad. Rumors of the Malachi prophecy would have spread like wildfire (summoning Wise men, perhaps?).

Even though I do think there is potential for a weird baby, I think Zacharias' words alone were enough to frighten the crowd:

[Luke 1:67] And his father Zacharias was filled with the Holy Ghost, and prophesied, saying,
[68]Blessed be the Lord God of Israel; for He hath visited and redeemed his people,

(Is this humor? Yes, Gabriel did visit, but so did the Christ. Yes, Jesus was an embryo, but Zacharias must have understood. "Dang, everybody, you just missed the IMPORTANT moment."

[69] And hath raised up an horn of salvation for us in the house of his servant David;

(Mary is not married. Joseph is not part of the story yet. Is this Zacharias identifying Mary as being from the House of David? Elizabeth seems to have Levite/Aaron credentials, which means Mary most likely also has "Daughter of Aaron" cred, but Zacharias mentions the other side of Mary's family tree with the House of David (a Judean). Remember this when Luke and Matthew list the family tree.

[70] As he spake by the mouth of his holy prophets, which have been since the world began:
[71] That we should be saved from our enemies, and from the hand of all that hate us;
[72] To perform the mercy promised to our fathers, and to remember his holy covenant;
[73] The oath which he sware to our father Abraham,
[74] That he would grant unto us, that we being delivered out of the hand of our enemies might serve him without fear,
[75] In holiness and righteousness before him, all the days of our life.

Previewing Baptism

Again, Zacharias shows an understanding that the Christ Plan began all the way back in the Garden of Eden, and that Adam and Eve did not wallow in their sin/guilt but "bought in" to the promise of the Christ, which was passed down to Noah, Abraham, King David, etc. etc. etc.

[76] And thou, child, shalt be called the prophet of the Highest: for thou shalt go before the face of the Lord to prepare his ways;

After nine months of pondering, Zacharias seems to be very clear on all of the Elijah/Christ prophecies. He clearly understands John's purpose on earth and connects it to the Elijah prophecy from Malachi. He also clearly understands that Christ will have a "face" and will walk around earth shortly after John fulfills his mission.

[Luke 1:77] To give knowledge of salvation unto his people by the remission of their sins,
[78] Through the tender mercy of our God; whereby the dayspring from on high hath visited us,

IE=Baptism. Peter repeats the phrase **"remission of sins"** in Acts 2 when he discusses Baptism. Here, Zacharias already knows what Wee John will do: he will baptize. This shows that John did NOT pick up the idea from Mandaeans while in Iraq. John was sent with the distinct purpose of preparing people to receive the Gospel from Christ. Also look at the phrase "dayspring." There are several OT references to a dayspring, but just the mere mention of water along with remission of sins gets me excited.

[79] To give light to them that sit in darkness and in the shadow of death, to guide our feet into the way of peace.

King David, despite his lustful addictions that plagued him while alive, seemed to understand the finer details about the purpose of the Christ, which Zacharias also seems to chase down. As modern Christians, we tend to celebrate the idea of getting an express ticket to Heaven because Jesus died on the cross for us. What about Adam? Abraham? Jacob? All of those "Heroes of Faith" died but did NOT go to Heaven. They all sat in "darkness." In Psalm 16, King David expresses his fears and joys about the Holy One. He understands his sins will bring death. He understands that "Sheol" waits for him because of this. But he also holds onto the promise that the Holy One will be coming for him.

This is the "Harrowing of Hell" concept that Zacharias also seems to anticipate. Zacharias finally understands the biggest picture possible that the Christ has come to redeem the living and the dead and will set everything right following the mess that happened in the Garden of Eden.

Reaching Anadeiknumi

[80] And the child grew, and waxed strong in spirit, and was in the deserts till the day of his shewing unto Israel.

Shewing? This strange Old English word left me as puzzled as the Greek word Anadeiknumi, which means exhibition, or public exhibition.

Let's back up a bit. So at birth, neighbors and relatives knew Wee John was different. From birth, Zacharias knew Wee John would baptize. Then he got stronger. Remember, the locals from (Bethany?) freaked out and began spreading the good news. We'll return to (Bethany?) in the Magi chapter, but let me just make a claim now: John was TOO POWERFUL to remain in Israel. The second half of this verse states that John was in the deserts UNTIL the day of his shewing.

What deserts? And why do we have more than one desert? Was John the Baptist a nomadic traveler?

If he pulled his punches for two decades, joined a religious order, got some training, and then went out to the Dead Sea for silent meditation for a bit, that would be a VERY ORDINARY JOHN (which he wasn't).

I believe John was raised "abroad" across the "deserts" and that is where his fame spread for many years. I believe it makes sense that he went as far as Parthia (Babylon/Iraq), which is why there are still Mandaeans who have a skewed view of this powerful prophet. I believe the "day of his shewing" is a reference to him turning thirty and then returning to Israel to preach. Remember, John is already famous but only lasts a few months before he gets arrested. How could a man this bold live for thirty previous years without stirring the pot? Those neighbors and relatives heard Zacharias and would have been a mob of zealous followers if John had stayed in Israel his entire life. This is the Prodigal Prophet returned!

Remember, Christianity was not just for the Jews. Salvation was intended for the Gentiles also. It makes sense that John prepared the way for Jesus in remote places like Parthia, Greece, Rome, and Turkey (even though I have no support for that theory). The deserts/wilderness reference could be anywhere beyond Israel.

Now, who turned 30 six months after John?

Yep, Jesus shows up at the Jordan River right after his birthday (Feast of Dedication), gets baptized, and begins His public exhibition.

CHAPTER EIGHT

HEIR TO THE PROMISE

If Mary was a virgin, does the backstory of Joseph even matter? After all, Jesus shares no DNA with him, right? No DNA. Here is an even more intriguing question: Does he share any DNA with Mary? Of course? Why did you say yes? Because in your mind, a baby comes from a man and a woman, and if Joseph wasn't the daddy, then God was the daddy and Mary was the mommy. Your assumption is that there needed to be a sexual relationship to end up with Jesus because, you know, science!

Yet God did not need a woman to create Adam, did he? He just spoke Adam into existence, and later, cloned Eve into existence by his Will and Word. God does not need to have sex with Mary, and just the thought disturbs me (but I do have a point to make). The Holy Ghost was male? Gabriel?

Can we just stop thinking like a human for a moment?

The Bible does not shy away from this being a miracle. It makes no sense and is quite impossible, right? (here's the turn in my point).

36 Begats Later

Then why did Matthew list the bloodline of Joseph? Cuz Joseph was his daddy!? Matthew clearly establishes that he believes it was a virgin birth that did not involve Joseph at all. If Matthew thinks this, why did he even bother listing 36 "begats" that connected Joseph to Abraham. It is NOT the bloodline of Jesus because Joseph was not involved.

Jesus is the heir of Joseph? That is Luke's point when he lists out the "son of" list. Jesus is the "son of" Joseph even though Joseph did not "beget" Jesus with Mary. Ah, but Zacharias said Mary was from the House of David, so Matthew lists her royal blood? Both Luke and Matthew end with the problematic inclusion of Joseph.

Throughout Jesus's ministries, strangers would glance at Jesus and understand that he was special, if not the Son of God (without much prompting). Was it his eyes? That distant yet personal gaze that modern actors use when playing Jesus? I don't know, but Matthew did know because Matthew saw Jesus. Consider this? With no Mary or Joseph DNA, Jesus could have looked much different than everyone else. What if he was given an Adam 1.0 model free of defects or genetic degradation?

(My point is still coming). I think Matthew included the "36 begat" list because Joseph was the fulfillment of God's promise to Abraham (and Adam and Eve). A promise was made back in the Garden of Eden that the Anointed One would come and save mankind. Matthew does not list out all 36 begats because Jesus is heir to a throne but because Joseph is heir to the promise.

This is a bloodline of believers. God has woven this bloodline through three thousand years of human history to arrive at Joseph, heir to the promise. God serves up the Christ Prophecy on a plate and delivers it to Joseph. Would Joseph (and humanity) be willing to accept the gift?

[Matthew 1:18] Now the birth of Jesus Christ was on this wise: When as his mother Mary was espoused to Joseph, before they came together,

See, Matthew clearly understands that M+J does not result in Jesus-the-Christ. Even though Matthew clearly establishes her virginity here, there is an insinuation that they might have "come together" at a later point in time, which is only troublesome if you want your Mary to be perpetually virgin.

A Jewish Wedding

Before we continue with the story of Mary arriving back in Nazareth, I'd first like to give you a bit of background on the Jewish wedding ceremony. It is hard for anyone to really know the ceremony used in Nazareth in the first century. If you think of weddings here in America, each is a bit different and way different than our parents, grandparents, or great-great grandparents, so I am reticent to put too much stock into the material I found.

I do think it is fascinating, so try to stick with me on this next page. The ceremony consists of three stages: contract, consummation, and celebration. Also, there is not really a ceremony in the synagogue like we have a wedding in a church.

Stage 1: Ketubbah

This is the contract stage. Unlike old systems in Europe, a Jewish bride would often be the one to initiate the process and choose her own husband. Once selected, the father of the bride would approach the groom with a contract to sign. Once signed, they were considered 100% married, even though they had not had sex yet. In this system, very young children were often married even though years would pass before things would move to the second stage.

Stage 2: Chuppah

The contract could be up to seven years in length. Part of the reason for this is so the groom could raise money for the contract. This is a bit like the dowry system. A groom's worth was proven by his ability to support and save up money for his bride. A father might set a high dollar amount to make sure the boy/groom is serious about his daughter. In other words, there were "cheap" girls out there by the dozen. Once the money is raised, the groom would return to the father of the bride and a date would be set. In preparation for the Chuppah, the bride would wait in something called the Chuppah room with her maids waiting outside. Once the deed was done, the maidens would retrieve the bloodied virginity cloth, which meant the deal was fulfilled by both parties.

Stage 3: Feast

After consummation, everyone goes to the groom's house for a party, and after the feast, the wedding ceremony is done.

That's how it was supposed to work, but sometimes things didn't go as planned. Divorce could be granted prior to Stage 3, which would have dissolved the contract and the groom would have been issued a refund for the payments he'd made. The Father-in-law would have the shame of having to give the money back and then having to go through the process again.

If the wife got pregnant prior to the Chuppah by the HUSBAND, then it was not really seen as a big deal since they were legally married anyway. It would have been a bit scandalous and also a downer (no party), but everyone would have been cool with it.

HOWEVER, if the woman got to the Chuppah Stage, and she was not a virgin, and the husband was NOT the baby-daddy, then a public stoning for adultery could happen. After all, if you let things go to the Chuppah Stage, then a bunch of people are already gathered. There would have been maidens who verified the woman was not a virgin and the groom and all of his guests would have been publically shamed. The Father-of-the-bride also would have been ruined by the moment because of the adultery violation. Even if he was a big dude with big sons, his daughter might have lived but been without any quality husbands to step up to the plate for her hand in marriage. Stoning would have ensued. So the reputation of a daughter would have been fiercely guarded by the Father of the Bride.

Joseph and Marriage

Let's take a moment now to ponder Joseph a bit before Matthew introduces him to the story. Earlier, I introduced Clopas and Mary, along with James the Just (who is murdered around

70 AD), Joses, Simeon, and Jude. Although there is not much to work with, it seems as if Joseph had a brother. My assumption was that Clopas was an older brother, but it certainly could be the other way around (James the Just would then be younger than Jesus which is problematic for him being an authority figure in the Book of Acts). If these cousins become "brothers," by the time of Christ's ministry, then something must have happened to Clopas (old age/murder?).

Is your mental image of Joseph that of an older man or a peer of Mary? If you've never thought of this, then great, you'll have an open mind. If you've made up your mind already, then let's explore both sides a bit before we continue with the greatest parenting team in the history of the world.

The Facts:

    A. No mention of Joseph during the ministry years

    B. Jesus "gives" his mother Mary to John (Disciple) at the cross.

    C. A reference to siblings of Jesus

    D. James the Just (cousin/bro) is killed around 70 AD

    E. Joseph was an Heir of David

    F. Joseph was known as a carpenter

    G. Joseph worked in Nazareth

    H. Joseph's lineage came from Bethlehem

The Old Joseph Theory (OJT):

Most people make a very logical assumption that since Joseph is not seen or hardly mentioned that he is dead during the ministry years. With the OJT, Joseph would be a man who acquired his education through his many years of life, and he also would have been a savvy, worldly guardian of baby Jesus during the dangerous years of Herod. The OJ would also have had wealth (to hide in Egypt) and social status as an honorable man. This also is supported when Jesus speaks to Mary and John (Disciple) on the cross and seems to pair them up for social/ministry care. If Mary was a widow, then somebody would have to take care of her, right? The OJT also would make Clopas a younger brother, and when Joseph died, Jesus became the ward of Clopas and brother to J,J,S,J and the girls. Speaking of the kids, I've seen OJT ideas that gave Joseph a previous wife who gave him JJ,S,J, and when he married Mary, he was so old that he did not long for a sexual relationship with her but only a little help with his 5+ kids. Mary the Nanny? I guess this theory would make Joseph an experienced father but would make the age of James the Just extremely old (Fact D) at the year 70 AD. The OJT would also support the idea that if Joseph the Heir is dead, then Jesus also becomes the legal heir to the Throne of David.

The Young Joseph Theory (YJT):

With this theory, Joseph would have more enthusiasm, strength, and zeal. He would have a certain tenderness. His worldliness would be a gift from the Holy Spirit. The YJT would make Clopas the older brother. If Clopas was older, Joseph would not be in line to own the family carpentry business. Like Andrew (Peter) and John the Disciple (James), he would be a second son whose life would either be that of field hand, or if he was smart, a candidate for religious training. A religiously trained Joseph does make sense, doesn't it? When Clopas dies, Joseph is suddenly back in the carpentry business and inherits

5+ kids and an adult woman (the other Mary) to care for. The YJ needs to work HARD to care for all of these people, which is an explanation on why we don't see him during the ministry years. With the YJT, Jesus is his firstborn son, which makes the dedication (Simeon/Anna) at the Temple required. A YJ would make him an heir of the Throne of David but not a direct heir and under the radar. With the YJT, Joseph would be 45-50 at the time of the Crucifixion, and Jesus "giving" Mary to John BD is not because she is a widow but because John needs to be trained. After all, John has a living mother, and Jesus has cousins (JJSJ+) to legally take care of his mother.

Do you see how both theories work?

Perhaps the only definitive proof I can offer to settle this debate is found in:

[Matthew 13:54] And when he was come into his own country, he taught them in their synagogue, insomuch that they were astonished, and said, Whence hath this man this wisdom, and these mighty works? [55] Is not this the carpenter's son? is not his mother called Mary? and his brethren, James, and Joses, and Simon, and Judas? [56] And his sisters, are they not all with us? Whence then hath this man all these things? [57] And they were offended in him. But Jesus said unto them, A prophet is not without honour, save in his own country, and in his own house. [58] And he did not many mighty works there because of their unbelief.

Is this not the carpenter's son? Dang! This present tense question makes it seem as if Joseph is still alive. Wasn't this…? Okay, so perhaps this is just an English translation issue, but how legendary of a carpenter was this guy that they know Jesus by his father's reputation. Of course, if Joseph had just died, then this would solve a few issues.

This verse also brings up the brothers and sisters, which seems to lock in the idea that Clopas was indeed the older brother. Why? James the Just is viewed as an authority figure by both Peter and Paul in the book of Acts as well as the Pharisees. Josephus writes that James the Just is a powerful spiritual leader for both Jew and Christian prior to the destruction of the Temple in 70 AD, and blames the murderers of James for bringing about the destruction of the city/temple. Yes, this would make James the Just 70-90 years old, but it would also make him old enough to be seen as wise in the Book of Acts.

The Trouble with Trimesters

Let's get back to the story. Through the years, I've seen all sorts of interpretations of the "discovery" of Mary being pregnant. All we have to guide us is a simple verse:

[Matthew 1:18] She was found with child of the Holy Ghost.

Remember, Mary was only three months pregnant and by all accounts was still a young woman. These two factors most likely mean that she was not showing (baby bump) at all. So regardless of her manner of return, there was no jealous, vindictive finger-pointing by the town tramp who hated Mary for being awesome and righteous.

What was her return like? Again, we are not given much to work with. When Gabriel visited, it seemed as if she was alone. It said she departed for the hill country (local hills/Judea) immediately. Yes, it was near an important holiday, but it does not indicate Mary being with anybody on her trip (which defeats the purpose of Gabriel's heads-up/warning). If immediately=without telling, then this might have resulted in a panic. Two families would have been freaking out: Mary's family, who missed their precious daughter, and Joseph and company, who lost an expensive fiancée. Did they search for her? Did they think she was abducted?

If she told everybody where she was going, then there would not have been much reason to discover her pregnancy so early. If it was a scheduled vacation, she could have returned to Nazareth at three-months pregnant and continued on with her life for quite a while. It seems strange to me that she was "found" to be pregnant when she was just three-months pregnant or else the public would have been able to see for themselves, right? No one but Mary's family and Joseph and company knew the truth. This is why I think it was an unexpected departure and an unexpected return. They would have wanted answers.

Apparently she told them, too.

No rape. No affair. She credits the Holy Ghost.

That is an eyebrow raising conversation, isn't it? Even if you are Joachim and Anna, and all the stuff from the ***Protevangelion*** and ***Gospel of the Birth of Mary*** was legit, it would still be incredible to hear. Does Mary have a "Moses glow" after her visit with the Trinity? Better yet…did Zacharias send guards? Don't scoff, think about it for a moment. If you are indeed not only a Kohen but possibly the unofficial high priest for all the Jews, do you not at minimum have a few trainees and graduate students at your disposal? If I am Zacharias, I would send a posse of armed guards to protect Mary all the way back to

Nazareth, and when she shows up at her home, I would have all thirty guards holding their knives and nodding with each sentence that comes out of Mary's mouth. Adultery? Stoning? You're going to have to go through my guards first!

If you want your Mary to sneak out of Bethany, then you must agree with me that she is so lit up by the Holy Spirit that they could see it on her face. Either way, she is believed (by her family).

Joseph's Options

How could Joseph have reacted? Based on her previously established lineage, intelligence, spiritual acuteness, and social standing, she would have fetched a very high Ketubbah. Joseph might have saved up his money for years to be able to buy into a marriage with a girl of this prominence. Regardless if she vanished or departed, he would have been quite anxious about his bride AND his investment.

Now, I like the idea of Joseph going into full-fledged hero mode when Mary vanishes. Did he involve his own family to join with Mary's family in searching for her? In modern day abductions, people go door-to-door, hanging fliers, and often personally search for the abducted. Could you go to the Roman authorities? They probably blamed the Roman authorities. Remember, Mary is already his legal wife, so he would have been quite invested in her safety.

Curiously, the Gospel of Luke does not even include this anecdote. Remember, Matthew was a local Galilean, and Luke was a physician that joined Team Jesus decades after these events. Once he became Team Jesus, it seems as if he used research to piece together his account. If Mary's return had been scandalous, then lots of local Galileans would have talked about how they had pregnant Mary all lined up in their sights, stone in hand, ready to kill her for adultery. Luke doesn't mention it, does he?

[Matthew 1:19] Then Joseph her husband, being a just man, and not willing to make her a public example, was minded to put her away privily.

Again, I think this verse establishes that Mary was not in any imminent danger by a stone wielding crowd because she was only 3 months pregnant. However, Joseph could have made it happen. Remember the Chuppah was meant to "inspect the goods" prior to marriage, and if Joseph suspected foul play, he could have Mary stoned for adultery. Less dramatic than that, he could just claim her as his wife a bit early. They were legally married, and simply waited to fulfill the details of the contract payments. He could have talked to Joachim and they could have been instantly declared husband and wife and aside from a feigned six-month pregnancy, no one would have known better.

Joseph does something quite curious to me. By privately dismissing this, he is about to lose a bunch of money. Whether old or young, Joseph walking away from the deal means Joachim keeps the dowry money. Publicly making her an example would mean he'd get to refund his money (but at the cost of her life).

Does Joseph think she's met somebody else (while in Judea) If so, he seems to be stepping aside to let her have true love. It also seems to indicate that Joseph was privately told by a member of Mary's family about the situation but he was not given all of the details.

[Matthew 1:20] But while he thought on these things, behold, the angel of the Lord appeared unto him in a dream,

Just a slight observation to make with this verse: Joseph was visited in a dream. On a scale of 1-10, with 10 being highest, Mary has not only stood before Gabriel, but at some point, she was "overshadowed" by God and the Holy Spirit. For Zacharias (probably a 9/10), he not only stood in the Holiest of Holies, but he also stood before Gabriel. Joseph, while described as a just man, was a mere mortal. Back in the day, Moses put rocks around Mount Horeb so that the Israelites wouldn't stand too closely and, you know, accidentally die. So Joseph is getting a "dialed down" encounter with just a dream.

[Matthew 1:20] saying, Joseph, thou son of David, fear not to take unto thee Mary thy wife: for that which is conceived in her is of the Holy Ghost. [21] And she shall bring forth a son, and thou shalt call his name JESUS: for he shall save his people from their sins. [22] Now all this was done, that it might be fulfilled which was spoken of the Lord by the prophet, saying, [23] Behold, a virgin shall be with child, and shall bring forth a son, and they shall call his name Emmanuel, which being interpreted is, God with us."

Now there is all sorts of cool stuff in this verse, but I'd like to point out something unique about Joseph. The angel quoted scripture. All the angel needed to say (if Joseph was an uneducated carpenter) was that the baby is from the Holy Ghost. Granted, this was just an 8/10 dream encounter, but it obviously would have made an impact. Instead, the angel also quotes a prophecy, which means Joseph must have known the prophecy. This is proof to me that Joseph isn't just naturally righteous but that he is also aware of scripture. The angel gave him a specific

Bible verse that meant something to Joseph. Joseph yearned for the Christ.

Also, notice the two names. Thou=Jesus. They=Emmanuel. Again, Joseph will use the name Jesus for the early years (keeping a secret), but later, the people of Israel will learn he is God incarnate, thus Emmanuel. This is a coy move by the angel, who is telling Joseph to keep the identity under wraps but that eventually everybody else will learn the child is the Christ.

[Matthew 1:24] Then Joseph being raised from sleep did as the angel of the Lord had bidden him, and took unto him his wife: [25] And knew her not till she had brought forth her firstborn son: and he called his name JESUS.

All of this is taking place at night=dream. So what Joseph does is quite irregular. What would Joachim and Anna think when Joseph knocks on their door at night? Danger? A stoning?

Does Mary have brothers? Are Zacharias' guards still there? When it turns out to be only Joseph, they surely must have expected a bit of legal drama, but instead, he told them about the dream.

What would Mary think at this point? Pretty romantic, huh? This guy believes her and wants to be a partner in this endeavor. Remember the Jewish Wedding process? Joseph throws all of that right out the window, doesn't he? By taking her as a wife, he brings her into his house. Yet there was no Chuppah or Feast. She was already legally his wife, but right then and there, with her dad present, Joseph claims her.

Yes, the people of Nazareth were robbed of a Feast. What was their assumption? "Guess he got her pregnant early, but her father was cool with it, so now they're husband and wife." A tiny bit scandalous, sure. A bit nontraditional, yes. Remember the reaction to learning the Christ came from Nazareth? Apparently, this place is not viewed as the righteous hub of Galilee. I'm not sure there were any angry villagers having to put down their stones. If Mary was being guarded by either her family or my Zacharias guards theory, Joseph walked in and basically told all of them, "I've got this."

CHAPTER NINE

CITY OF DAVID

So between Matthew 1:25 and Luke 2:1, nothing happens (or nothing is recorded). We leave off with Mary going into the house of Joseph and then continue the story in her ninth month of pregnancy with the trip to Bethlehem. While the trip to Bethlehem is certainly amazing and the heart of the nativity story, I'd like to pause to contemplate the reality of those missing six months.

Summer School

It's hard to imagine either Mary or Joseph winning the Christ lottery if they didn't come from righteous stock. The marriage expectations combined with the dramatic "claiming" of Mary by Joseph in the middle of the night certainly would have made it a topic of interest for her family, and more likely than not, Joseph's family would have at least inquired why there wasn't going to be a party. I have to assume both families would have gained a little insight into the situation.

So what does Joseph do on Monday morning? Seriously! How would you go to work the next day if you knew Mary carried the Christ child? Remember, both of them have had some pretty intense God moments involving angels, signs, and being "overshadowed." Now that these two have come together, they would begin sharing their stories. For Joseph, it would be an explanation of his dream encounter with an angel, and for Mary, she'd have to explain her warning encounter, her "overshadowed" moment, and her encounter with John, Elizabeth, and Zacharias. So work on Monday morning? Doubtful.

So how would you spend these six months? With a supportive family, you could lay low. If they were believers, this would be possible. A protective Joseph certainly would rather die than leave her unattended. How could you EVER just go back to your routine?

But you'd need to form a game plan. Within the first week of wonder, an obvious solution would emerge…study scripture. Think about some Christians you know (possibly yourself) and the amount of time dedicated to reading the Bible. With a bit of inspiration from the Holy Spirit and a lot of second-hand accounts, we SHRED chapter and verse with only our own salvation on the line. Mary and Joseph had the fate of the world in their hands. These two kids would get serious rather quickly, wouldn't they?

Based on Mary's song, I think she has the ability to have access to scripture, but Joseph is a bit more mysterious. If he is a "second son," then he might have some training. Another possibility is a big assist from the Holy Spirit, who could just "reveal" the truth to them. Do they seek out a reverent scribe or Pharisee

that can be trusted? Would the families go find a series of scholars? Remember, if you knew the Christ was next door, what ex-
expense would you spare?

Google "Old Testament Christ Prophecies" and you can find
hundreds and hundreds of passages flagged for some connection.
And these are just the commonly accepted connections. Mary
and Joseph, with access to the scriptures, could have spent each
day of those next six months discovering and discussing those
passages.

If it were me, I'd be terrified. I would frantically seek answers
about what was going to happen and what needed to happen.
I'd make lists and lists of verses so I could be prepared. I'd be the
best Christ expert I could possibly be.

Would they have been a bit confused when they read about
verses indicating the origins of the Christ had connections to
Nazareth, Bethlehem, and Egypt. Certainly. Did they believe in
Fate or Free Will? Free Will would have led Joseph to make a
choice for where to bring Mary for the birth. Fate would have
led Joseph to let it happen as God intended.

So imagine how excited they would have been when this
happened:

> **[Luke 2:1] And it came to pass in those days, that there went
> out a decree from Caesar Augustus, that all the world should
> be taxed. [2](And this taxing was first made when Cyrenius
> was governor of Syria.) [3] And all went to be taxed, every one
> into his own city."**

Did the Romans commonly tax? Of course. Did the Romans
commonly conduct a census? Um, no. Is it weird to require

them to go to their "heritage" towns? It's a trap! (Admiral Ackbar voice).

Sensing the Trap

How would Mary and Joseph have seen this decree? Part of them must have understood it to be fulfillment of prophecy. After all, if the Pharisees in Jerusalem could figure out that the Christ child was supposed to come from Bethlehem, then certainly Mary and Joseph, lit by the spirit, would have known already.

But Joseph must have also known it was a trap. How could you not see it as a trap? The research on this time period is quite sloppy (at best), but I did read that this census focused on "Jews of High Rank." If Herod and/or the Romans wanted to eliminate the Christ prophecy, they could use the Jews' love of lineage against them. Now remember, the House of David was a big mess, so lots of Jews could connect themselves to one of David's many children (legit and illegitimate). Once the list was complete…?

Now I'm not sure whether this census would be pushed by Herod or the Romans (perhaps both), but they would have needed the right man to pull it off. So who was this governor of Syria?

Who's Running this Show?

Again, history is pretty sloppy here, and there are a lot of experts with different twists on the accuracy of Luke. Now, Luke could be looking back (from the 4th decade A.D.) and remember that Cyrenius (also known historically as Quirinius) was responsible for the census. Historically, the problem is that Quirinius was NOT the Roman governor of Syria during this time—it was Varus.

Publius Quinctillius Varus was a "connected" Roman that held all sorts of important titles. A few years prior to Jesus being born (4 B.C.), Varus was governor of Africa. Right before Jesus was born, Varus became the governor of Syria from 7 BC-4 BC. Around the time of Jesus' birth, Varus went back to Rome. He's not really famous for any of these posts he held. What gained him fame was that he was next posted to Germania, where he lost three Roman legions to a man history would dub Herman the German. That's right, Varus is an epic failure.

What about Quirinius? Well this guy really did conduct a census, but it came much later in the years 6-7 AD. I know the calendar/year system is a bit of a mess (thus 4 BC=Jesus born), but this cannot explain such a big problem.

Here's what I found that makes the most sense to me. Varus was a mediocre governor that did not handle turmoil well. In the year prior to Jesus' birth, there was turmoil in Judea. Why? Well, news of a messiah spread to all corners of the region. There were most likely signs and omens besides all the rumors leaking. According to records and historic commentary, there were all sorts of revolts about the time Mary and Joseph were leaving for Bethlehem. Plus, Varus was supposed to have completed the census by 8-7 BC. He was already late. Varus needed to do something.

Guess what Quirinius was good at? Quirinius spent the previous decade fighting guerillas in two hostile regions. So when a "messianic revolt" broke out, who better to help quell it than Quirinius. While Varus sat in Damascus, Quirinius and his men were out dealing with rebel scum and fixing the mess made by Varus. Remember, Varus is fired about the time Jesus is born, which means he did not do his job well. The census (Varus) failed. The suppression of the rebels (Quirinius) did not fail. For all intents and purposes, Quirinius was the acting governor sent to clean things up while Varus was the official governor (who got canned). This is just one of many ways to wiggle out of the governor problem.

A Convenient Excuse

So let's get back to Mary and Joseph.

[Luke 2:4] And Joseph also went up from Galilee, out of the city of Nazareth, into Judaea, unto the city of David, which is called Bethlehem; (because he was of the house and lineage of David:) [5] To be taxed with Mary his espoused wife, being great with child.

My assumption is that Joseph must have known the prophecies about the Christ being born in Bethlehem because why else would he take Mary. This is monumentally dumb unless he wanted her to give birth along the way (and I don't think Joseph is dumb).

There are a couple other things to consider about why he brought Mary along. First, perhaps she is also from the lineage of David. I know, this certainty doesn't seem like a sexist Roman thing to do (registering the women) but maybe. Second, look at the timing. 'Tis the Season for…the Feast of Dedication. Long before Christmas, the Feast of Dedication had been a wintry excuse to travel to Jerusalem. Remember, Mary and Joseph certainly come from devout Jewish stock, so making three trips a year to Jerusalem is common place. If you have to go to Bethlehem because of the Romans, why not make it convenient and wait until you had a good reason to go.

The previous few pages established that this "census" was not done quickly, so your mental picture of Romans rousting people from their sleep is probably a misconception. If it indeed was a big trap (meant to get a kill list for later purposes (cough) Domitian), then the Romans would dress it up as a requirement but, you know, take care of it sooner than later (so as not to freak everybody out). Mary and Joseph could discreetly slip down to Bethlehem to "do their duty" to the Romans.

In the movies, this is often where they show Mary and Joseph struggling to get through roaring rivers and crossing deserts.

Um? Highways!

The King's Highway was a centuries old trade route that ran north-to-south along the coastal flatlands of Israel. It stretched from as far south as Aksum (Ethiopia) and went as far as China. From Nazareth, you travel just a few miles west (all downhill) and then it is a major interstate road certainly patrolled by Romans or Jews (think CHIPS on donkeys), especially during a major holiday like the Feast of Dedication. The passage would have been public and reasonably comfortable.

Are you picturing Mary and Joseph walking alone? Why? We've already established that Clopas has a family, and Mary certainly also had kin. Heck, the entire village of Nazareth might have all set off together in one big caravan. There is no reason to be alone, and if it does line up with the Feast of Dedication, then they certainly had others with them.

[Luke 2:6] And so it was, that, while they were there, the days were accomplished that she should be delivered.

While…

If I'm right, they came for the Feast of Dedication. Today, this festival is celebrated as "Hanukkah" but it is pretty much the same thing as it was then…the Festival of Lights. For Mary and Joseph it was a well-established tradition that went back to the days of the Maccabee rebellion. An evil dude by the name of Antiochus Epiphanes (lil' Antichrist #5. Another pitch for my End Times book) desecrated the temple, which led to a rebellion by the Jews. This happened in Chislev (our December), and after a bunch of fighting, the Jews retook the Temple on (dramatic pause)…the 25th of Chislev.

Even though the Jewish calendar shifts the date around within the month of December, the first one began on the 25th. The miracle is that the rebels only found a small amount of oil for the menorah, but it ended up lasting eight days. Look at all the symbolism here. Seven Days of Creation + one. Jesus is the light. Heavy stuff.

For Mary and Joseph, regardless of the exact day they arrived in Jerusalem, they would have wanted to celebrate the Feast of Dedication with their friends and relatives, right? ***While*** implies a bit of a vacation. ***When*** implies it happened immediately. Your mental movie probably has Mary going into labor on the outskirts of Bethlehem, but to get there, they had to stop by Jerusalem first.

Travel Plans

It seems quite reasonable that Mary and Joseph would have planned to stay for the Feast of Dedication, which meant regular housing. Who to stay with? WHY NOT stay with Zacharias and Elizabeth in nearby (Bethany). They certainly would have had a lot of catching up to do. It would have been a chance for them to meet John the Elijah (now six months old and calling fire down from the sky? Toddlers!) Mary and Joseph "made camp" when they arrived.

More likely than not, they probably went into Jerusalem for the Feast of Dedication also. Although I'm not sure on when The Festival of Lights fell in 4BC, I'm betting they arrived around Dec 18th or so. If so, then they would have gone into town for the lighting ceremony, listened to Zacharias preach, and generally hung out in Bethany.

A Three-Hour Tour

Eventually, Joseph would have had to make an interesting decision: when to go to Bethlehem to get registered. Remember, they most likely have a posse with them. Some would have sensed a trap by Herod and/or the Romans. Mary would have chided them and talked about Grace. Finally, it was probably decided that Mary and Joseph would go alone (to avoid attention) to Bethlehem.

> **[Luke 2:7] And she brought forth her firstborn son, and wrapped him in swaddling clothes, and laid him in a manger; because there was no room for them in the inn.**

Surprise! Their little three-hour trip to Bethlehem got really complicated when she went into labor. Why no room in the inn? The Feast of Dedication!!!

Now, think of the Palm Sunday scene. Remember how Jesus told his disciples not to sweat the details, and sure enough, there was a donkey ready for his use. Mary and Joseph might have expected a grandiose God moment to happen in Bethlehem where the richest man in town with three midwives opened his house to them, but that's not *this* story, is it? It is all about humility.

Regarding the Manger

Cave or stable?

There are LOTS of fun theories about the exact room conditions for baby Jesus, but it really doesn't matter much. I've read that the Jewish "inn" would have had human quarters on the top floor and a stable on the bottom floor. That works. I've also read that around Bethlehem, there are little caves in the hills and mountains. The great matriarch Rachel was placed in one of these caves. Apparently, there is strong support for animals being kept in such a cave. That works too. Buried in some zany Pseudepigraphal works, there is even an old story about Satan trying to kill Adam and Eve with a big boulder, which turns into a protective dome (which they stay in for 3 days) and once they are let out, it becomes the same cave Mary and Joseph find the manger. That works too.

Personally, I'd pick a cave for the privacy of my wife giving birth, but who knows what Joseph picked.

Now, at the same time Mary was giving birth, this was happening:

[Luke 2:8] And there were in the same country shepherds abiding in the field, keeping watch over their flock by night.

So same country certainly implied Judea, and most likely, the hills by Bethlehem. Since Jesus will be a shepherd for his disciples, God once again gets an A for his use of symbolism.

The Heavenly Host

And, lo, the angel of the Lord came upon them, and the glory of the Lord shone round about them: and they were sore afraid.

It really doesn't matter, but is your angel flying above them or walking up beside them? I also wonder "which" angel this happens to be.

And the angel said unto them, Fear not: for, behold, I bring you good tidings of great joy, which shall be to all people. [11] For unto you is born this day in the city of David a Savior, which is Christ the Lord. [12] And this shall be a sign unto you; Ye shall find the babe wrapped in swaddling clothes, lying in a manger.

Obviously, this angel is quite excited. It makes me wonder if he was "sent" by God or if he just showed up on his own. Take a look at Zechariah 1:12, and you will see the same "Angel of the Lord" asking God how long he had to wait. While *angel* means *malak*, which means messenger, it makes me wonder how much divine preparation God gave his angels. Instead of focusing on this scene from the shepherd/human perspective, think of it from the angels. You've been neck deep in the sinful mess created long ago in the garden, and except for the Great Flood and

Sodom and Gomorrah, you've been on the sideline while God lets humans sort things out for themselves. The big fix? The Christ! But for four thousand years, this promise has not come. Now that it has come, the angels had to be stoked! Remember this, because thirtyish years later, when Jesus is on the cross, things go screwy when he dies. Curtains rip, darkness covers the sky, the earth quakes, and the dead rise out of Sheol. If the angels were "in on it," they certainly didn't act like it. In Revelation 12:10, you'll see the same zealous excitement when the angels "brothers" accept the promise of Christ's salvation (Flashback? Foreshadow?). Perhaps angels are just excitable.

Perhaps these shepherds are the first few dominoes of evangelizers and believers, and like Mary and Joseph, God predetermined them to have a specific part.

[Luke 2:13] And suddenly there was with the angel a multitude of the heavenly host praising God, and saying,
[14] Glory to God in the highest, and on earth peace, good will toward men."

Cool, huh? These angels obviously are up in the sky, giving the shepherds, and anybody else nearby, quite a show. Unfortunately, the villains would have noticed this also (Com'n man, be cool). However, I have a bit of a strange theory to pass on involving Psalm 91.

<u>Psalm 91 Rules(!)</u>

Psalm 91 is popular for various reasons, but I LOVE it for its use in the Satan/Temptation in the Wilderness anecdote. Now, I firmly believe that when Jesus went to Satan in the wilderness, he had fully become God on Earth, even if Satan didn't know it quite yet. At the baptism scene, God had already congratulated Jesus and also sent down the Holy Spirit. Next step…prepare the disciples. But before Jesus gathered up his church, he went out into the wilderness, and like a teacher spying on class with a substitute teacher, God sees the evil lies of Satan with his own (Jesus) eyes.

In the course of being tempted, Jesus uses the words of Moses to defend himself against Satan's temptations. Nice work, Mary and Joseph. Yet Satan also seems to know the "rules" about the Christ from what Moses wrote down. If you think of the Book of Job, it seems as if Satan is referencing the rules of engagement for the Christ in the same way he had rules of engagement for Job.

So let's do a quick overview of Psalm 91.

- Moses addresses Jesus, who in 14th century BC, is still up in Heaven.
- Moses declares his trust in the Christ
- Moses writes the Psalm, which will be read by Jesus, saying…
- God will deliver you (Jesus) from Satan.
- God will protect you (Jesus) with his wings (Holy Spirit)
- Bad guys can't hurt you.
- Lots of people will die around you (Bethlehem infants)
- But Satan won't be allowed near you.
- However, you will be exposed to evil (living in Nazareth)
- Yet Moses knows Jesus won't sin.
- As the Christ, Jesus can command the angels to provide assistance…
- If any of the symbolic evils challenge him while on earth.

- Moses is stoked because he knows that his words/books will be used by the Christ to defeat Satan, and in turn, Jesus will come and get him from Sheol (at the Transfiguration)

Don't think this verse is about the Christ? Then why did Satan quote it? It was a challenge of ego/pride for Jesus to abuse his power.

So here is my point. Yes, the angels spreading out over the shepherds was certainly pretty, but what was the purpose? A Holy Kazoo moment?

"Under the shadow of the Almighty" and **"cover you with His feathers"** seem to imply that the Christ will be divinely protected. What if the angels that appeared above the shepherds were sentries being sent out to keep supernatural villains like Satan away from baby Jesus so that the "worth" of humanity can be decided by letting Him grow up with regular sin and temptation around him? These angels spread out as a shield and net to keep Satan away (for up to 30 years).

When Jesus passed the test and was baptized, he brought his first disciples home/to his mom, and then walked TO Satan, who was way out in the wilderness. Why did Jesus walk so far? Because he had to be the one to walk away from the protection of the Almighty. Jesus went to Satan (and passed another test).

[Luke 2:15] And it came to pass, as the angels were gone away from them into heaven, the shepherds said one to another, Let us now go even unto Bethlehem, and see this thing which is come to pass, which the Lord hath made known unto us. [16] And they came with haste, and found Mary, and Joseph, and the babe lying in a manger.

It's hard to mess this moment up in the movies, but I really do wonder HOW the shepherds knew where to go. Remember, Bethlehem is packed for the Feast of Dedication. If you think of it practically, there were a lot of crying babies in Bethlehem, yet all the shepherds had to go on was a "manger" reference. So let's go check the stables, guys. How many stables did they have to check? Did they receive supernatural spotlights indicating where the baby could be found? If so, that is a bit reckless for a world filled with human villains.

> **[Luke 2:17] And when they had seen it, they made known abroad the saying which was told them concerning this child. [18] And all they that heard it wondered at those things which were told them by the shepherds. [19] But Mary kept all these things, and pondered them in her heart. [20] And the shepherds returned, glorifying and praising God for all the things that they had heard and seen, as it was told unto them.**

How "abroad" did they go? Was this just a local flyby of the hills, or did they go to another country entirely?

Regardless, there certainly would have been a buzz in the country, and Herod was certain to have heard about it.

CHAPTER TEN

TWO GIVING FIGS

Before we get to Herod and talk about Jerusalem, let's spend a little time going over the background behind the date of Christmas. At a quick glance, it seems pretty arbitrary. Nothing clearly states when Jesus was born. In fact, early Christians used to view birthdays as a pagan practice, thus beneath them. Now, it is certainly worthy to commemorate the Nativity, but those who would have known the details about Jesus' birth would not have bothered to bake a cake, light the candles, and exchange birthday presents.

It just wasn't a thing.

It also doesn't mention the season of his birth. Do I think it fits with the Feast of Dedication? Yes, but it simply does not say it 'on the record,' does it?

I've read shepherd theories also, but having raised sheep myself, I can remember "tending my flock" 24/7/365, so that doesn't help much either.

So how did we end up with December 25th?

There are three excellent Biblical points that support a winter birthday, but before we get to those, let's get all of the ick out of the way.

Saturnalia

Ick #1: Saturnalia. For those of you who have avoided the horror series "The Purge," let me explain. Saturnalia is a Roman holiday that begins with debauchery and ends in human sacrifice. It was a weeklong ordeal, beginning on December 17th and ending on December 25th. This bizarre ritual existed for centuries prior to Jesus and seemed to exist at some level for a while after Jesus. While the Catholic Church was born in Rome, Christianity existed throughout the Roman empire and then some. Some speculate that the Roman Catholics just merged two holidays together, but pagan and Christian ceremonies could easily have coexisted for quite a while.

Antiochus Epiphanes Birthday

Ick #2: Long before the Romans possessed the Holy Lands, the Persians and Greeks held it. As I mentioned in the previous chapter, the Feast of Dedication came about because Seleucid Emperor Antiochus Epiphanes was flat out evil and wanted a bloodbath. He knew the trigger for the Jews would be the desecration of the Temple, so that's what he did. A riot broke out that turned into a war. Things didn't go as expected. Some stories say that Antiochus Epiphanes' birthday was December 25th, so this outrageous act was both personal and strategic.

Ick #3: Before he dubbed himself Antiochus Epiphanes, he was born Mithridates. The Persians worshipped a god named Mithras, and celebrated him on…you guessed it, December 25th.

So yes, there are three icky things associated with the date, but isn't it just like evil to try to muddy up something good. That is why I think the Festival of Lights is so cool, because the Maccabee boys gave evil the middle finger on December 25th, turning it from a dark holiday (Mithras) into a…light holiday (sorry about the pun).

So let's build a case for keeping Christmas on the 25th:

Speculation #1: The Zacharias timeline.

This all hinges on Zacharias being a "high priest" and performing his rites in "THE" Temple on the Feast of Tabernacles. You can easily pull at the strings of this argument, but I love the timeline it supports. First, the Feast of Tabernacles would take place around September. Add six months onto that, and Mary conceives right around the time of the Passover (awesome symbolism. Another A+). This means that John was born around June (St. John's birthday is celebrated in June). Add six months onto June and you have…December. See how fun that was?

Speculation #2: The Baptism Timeline.

This theory needs to be counted both backwards and forwards. The Book of John gives specific days from Jesus being baptized to the wedding in Cana (but then no mention of the

Temptation in the Wilderness). John's next anecdote is placed at the Passover in Jerusalem. If you add up the two anecdotes, you start with

Passover=March

-40 days walking into the Wilderness

-40 days walking out of the Wilderness

-3 or 4 days walking to Cana from the Baptism

=?

That's right, approximately ninety days prior to being at the Passover, Jesus was visiting Jerusalem during the Feast of Dedication. The significance? Regarding John the Baptist, it clearly states that he returned to Judea when he turned 30. Apparently, the Bar Mitzvah is a new, fourteenth century Jewish custom, and before that, a "man" waited until his thirtieth birthday before he was given "voice" in adult matters, such as publically reading scripture in the synagogue. If John returned in June, he had several months to rile up the local authorities. If John returned when he turned thirty, then six months later, Jesus turned 30 also. Jesus gets baptized right after his birthday, folks. THEN his ministry begins.

Speculation #3: Herod's Death.

The historians are pretty solid on this detail (please excuse Pope Gregory). Okay, let's first explain the Gregorian calendar. Gregory wanted to count the years since Jesus' birth. You know, B.C./A.D. To him, everything changed when Jesus was born (why not count down from his death then?) Unfortunately, the calendar got really messed up when experts realized that Caesar Octavius was the same guy as Caesar Augustus (the Artist Formerly known as Octavius). Octavius changed his name four years into his reign. Gregory's guys thought they were two different rulers. Because of this gaff, ALL of the dates that had just been recalculated were off by 4 years! So Jesus technically was born in 4 BC!

Thanks to Roman and Jewish records, we know exactly when Herod died…March 13th. You see, there was an eclipse in the sky that day and also, well…people wrote it down, along with Herod's death. Remember, Mary and Joseph fled to Egypt to escape the wrath of Herod, and then an angel came and told them it was safe to go back home. If Herod were a psychopath, then he would have continued to hunt them down if he heard any rumors. A quick trip to Egypt makes sense.

__Meet King Herod__

Let's take some time to discuss old Herod for a while, because while Mary and Joseph were meeting the Shepherds, Herod was probably noticing the angels in the skies above Bethlehem.

In 74 B.C. (Thanks, Gregory, now my head hurts) Herod was born in Idumaea (south of Judea) and was a Judaized Edomite (remember Lot and his daughters? No? That's because most Sunday school classes avoid talking about incest between father and daughter, especially one that creates an entire nation. Edomites were the ultimate hillbillies to the Jews. So he had a bit of Jew in him but mostly he was an outsider).

At the age of 25, Herod was appointed Governor of Judea because of his close relationship with Rome. The Sanhedrin didn't like him, and when the Parthians dethroned him, he fled back to Rome. While in Rome, the Senate gave him the title

"King of the Jews" and when he returned in 37 BC, he married the Jewish princess Mariamne to seal the deal.

I'm your new king!

As King of Judea, he played a critical role in the Roman civil wars. Initially, he allied himself with Mark Anthony and Cleopatra of Egypt, but he quickly changed sides to favor the Caesar formerly Known as Octavius (Augustus). As a reward for his loyalty, he was given a force of 2,000 foreign secret police and the friendship of Rome. He immediately became a great builder, restoring the Temple of Solomon, building a harbor at Caesarea, the fortress of Masada, and a pagan shrine at Paneas (Caesarea Philippi).

Oh yeah, he was a psycho killer, also.

Yep, he killed wives, sons, and anyone else that threatened his power. After five marriages, he had evil heirs all over the place. If he were willing to kill his own sons to secure his throne, how would he react to news of a messiah being born nearby?

Meet the Monkey

Even though the name Caiaphas belongs to the Easter story, it is more likely than not that he was around during this same time period. Remember, thirty years after Jesus was born, this guy was firmly entrenched as the Roman appointed "High Priest."

During Herod's reign, Shimon Ben Boethus was the high priest, a man with old bloodlines. Just like today, there were social liberals and conservatives in Jerusalem. Pharisees were old school; Sadducees were more "Greek" in attitude. So too were the religious families grasping for power. Bet Shammai was considered the "conservative" house while Bet Hillel was viewed to be the "liberals."

Caiaphas would have been a young man at this time, born into the Kuppai family. Never heard of them? That was the problem. Caiaphas earned the nickname "the monkey" after publically opposing Mishnat-Hasidim. His next move was much more successful. He married the daughter of Annas Bar Seth, who was poised for a power play. Remember, Quirinius was called into Syria to help put down an uprising by rebels, and Governor Varus is credited with putting down a religious uprising at the same time period.

Well, guess what happened in 4 BC? (Me, me, me…Jesus was born!) Annas Bar Seth deposed Herod's former High Priest and sets up his family (and son-in-law) for a run that would last all the way up to the year 63 AD. Makes you wonder what made Herod change his mind?

As you can imagine, even during the Festival of Lights, Jerusalem was a scary place to visit.

Next Step: Circumcision

Let's get back to Mary and Joseph for a while now. We know with certainty Jesus was born in Bethlehem, but we do not know how long they stayed, do we? Did Joseph ever go down to the registration station? Did the pregnancy interrupt this? Well, we do know she gave birth, and Jesus spent at least one night in a manger. Then what? If I were Joseph, I would want to get the Christ out of the manger as soon as possible, which means he had to politely wait at least a few days for Mary to rest.

Did their families worry? Again, if they traveled with others, did the others come looking for them? They must have known where they went. Zacharias certainly would have been worried and then stunned when the Bethlehem prophecy came true. Let's give Mary a few extra days and say they waited in Bethlehem for five days. Then what?

Back to Nazareth?

While it would make sense to go home, you must remember that Jesus was a firstborn son. There were religious rules and expectations. Jesus needed to be circumcised.

[Luke 2:21] And when eight days were accomplished for the circumcising of the child, his name was called JESUS, which was so named of the angel before he was conceived in the womb.

Okay, I would not want to be the guy with the blade, but since the days of Genesis, circumcision was a holy ritual. Who would I take baby Jesus to see? Well, Zacharias seems pretty obvious, doesn't it? He is a holy man and a relative. Perfect.

One thing I know for certain is that he did NOT live in Bethlehem, or else there would have been room for Mary and Joseph somewhere in town. Although only speculative, Bethany still makes sense to me based on the "Lazarus friendship" situation. Bethany is only a few miles from Bethlehem and Jerusalem, so when Mary did agree to travel, the trip would have lasted only a few hours before she could rest.

IF the Feast of Dedication happened to begin on December 25th, all of the religious pilgrims would have left Jerusalem eight days later. Nice coincidence, right? Now that Jesus is circumcised, they can head back home to Nazareth, right?

Next Step: The Temple

Unfortunately, there were a few more religious conventions, and since Jesus was not only male but also a firstborn, he needed to be dedicated at the Temple.

[Luke 2:22] And when the days of her purification according to the law of Moses were accomplished, they brought him to Jerusalem, to present him to the Lord; [23] (As it is written in the law of the Lord, Every male that openeth the womb shall be called holy to the Lord;) [24] And to offer a sacrifice according to that which is said in the law of the Lord, A pair of turtledoves, or two young pigeons.

So they're kinda stuck in Judea for the next 32 days. If they were regular folks (which they are NOT), they would have certainly rushed home and done this at the next Festival (like Passover in March). If they are staying with family, in a house, then why not spend more time with Zacharias and Elizabeth. Certainly, Zacharias would have been honored to spend a few weeks with his Messiah. How would you say no to this request?

A Sign For Simeon

Forty days after Jesus was born, Mary could have brought him into the Temple. Imagine the fear and excitement they must have felt bringing Jesus into the big city. They probably wanted to keep their heads low and just get it over with. Instead, the opposite happened:

[Luke 2:25] And, behold, there was a man in Jerusalem, whose name was Simeon; and the same man was just and devout, waiting for the consolation of Israel: and the Holy Ghost was

upon him. [26] And it was revealed unto him by the Holy Ghost, that he should not see death, before he had seen the Lord's Christ. [27] And he came by the Spirit into the temple: and when the parents brought in the child Jesus, to do for him after the custom of the law, [28] Then took he him up in his arms, and blessed God, and said,

[29] Lord, now lettest thou thy servant depart in peace, according to thy word: 30 For mine eyes have seen thy salvation, [31] Which thou hast prepared before the face of all people; [32] A light to lighten the Gentiles, and the glory of thy people Israel. [33] And Joseph and his mother marveled at those things which were spoken of him. [34] And Simeon blessed them, and said unto Mary his mother, Behold, this child is set for the fall and rising again of many in Israel; and for a sign which shall be spoken against; [35] (Yea, a sword shall pierce through thy own soul also,) that the thoughts of many hearts may be revealed.

How awesomely horrible was that? Not that Mary and Joseph needed any more confirmation about their baby being the Christ, but hey, some stranger came right up and verified it. Dang! Remember the desire for privacy? Well, this old guy Simeon, regardless of his intentions, just put a big target on your back only a few blocks away from psychopaths like Herod and Caiaphas (not to mention the Romans, too). Gee, thanks, Simeon. We know. And what about all that cryptic talk at the end? Swords shall pierce your soul? I sure hope that is a metaphor. There is also quite a bit of beauty in his words, especially if this just took place after the Festival of Lights.

I'm sure Mary and Joseph wanted to bolt, but before they could leave for home or return to "the house" of Zacharias and Elizabeth, another special moment happens.

The Recognition of Anna

[Luke 2:36] And there was one Anna, a prophetess, the daughter of Phanuel, of the tribe of Asher: she was of a great age, and had lived with an husband seven years from her virginity; [37] And she was a widow of about fourscore and four years, which departed not from the temple, but served God with fastings and prayers night and day. [38] And she coming in that instant gave thanks likewise unto the Lord, and spake of him to all them that looked for redemption in Jerusalem.

All sorts of awesome here, also. First, the fact that Anna exists is a miracle. Now, I'm not talking about her age (but that is quite impressive for the time period). She comes from the Tribe of Asher. Now, in case you don't know, the Twelve Tribes broke up shortly after King Solomon stole the throne from his brother. Israel became the term for the 10 northern tribes, and Judea became the term for the two southern tribes, Judah and Benjamin. When Assyria grew strong, it flexed its muscles by annihilating the northern kingdom, selling the survivors into slavery, essentially erasing the tribes from the map. Centuries later, while the tribe of Judah flourishes still as the Jews of the Holy Lands, Anna shows up representing the tribe of Asher. That's cool. She, like her tribe, has been through a lot, and as a reward, she gets to see the Christ before she dies.

Both Anna and Simeon also reinforced what I assume Mary and Joseph knew well by this point: the purpose of the Christ. Heck, Simeon all but said Mary's heart would be broken.

Keep the camera rolling.

Anna gives the baby back, and now what?

Are Mary and Joseph packed, ready to return to Nazareth? Luke seems to imply that, because he jumps right into a verse about going back to Nazareth (cuz that's where Jesus grew up, right Luke?). Luke also refers to Mary and Joseph "performing all things" required of them. Bethlehem birth? Check. Circumcised? Check. Presented at the Temple? Check. Wowed some old folks? Double Check. Anything left to fulfill, Joseph?

Um…the Magi?

(did Luke forget to mention that?)

CHAPTER ELEVEN

GIFTS OF THE WISE MEN

What is a Wise Man? Before we look at the story of the Wise Men, or Magi as they are often called, let's just explore the word a bit. While Wise Men is an English euphemism of sorts, the term Magi has all sorts of meaning to different cultures.

The Latin word Magi (or singular Magus) eventually became the source for the word Magician, which has all sorts of occult connotations, thus Wise Men sounds less witchy. For example, Simon the Magus from the Book of Acts was an evil Samaritan sorcerer more interested in buying power than reforming his corrupt ways. Wise Man.

The Greeks have the word Magos, the Kurds have the word Manji, and the Persians used Magus. Didn't they come from the East? Isn't Persia…east? For all intents and purposes, Daniel was a Magi in the court at Babylon, working side by side with the other pagan Magi. Okay, so I'm cool with Magi. Seems historical.

I've seen research arguing that the word Astrologers or Astronomers could also be used, because, you know…star. And if you put together the Persia/Babylon connection that is so obvious in the use of "east" and match it up with what was going on in the Babylon area, then Magi, Wise Men or even Astro Men seem to work.

Yet even in Persia, the definition is not very tight. Mag-Men have four possible meanings and origins even in Persia.

First, they could be a follower of Zoroaster (shudder). If true, then they were indeed Astro-men, who not only studied the stars but also were a priestly order. They also had connections with magic, through ancestry with the Chaldeans and Medes.

Second, this meaning could have nothing to do with foreign religions but could refer to an ethnic group. This "younger" Avestan word would thus refer to a tribe in western Iran (which would still be east of Judea).

Third, Herodotus writes of Iranian expatriates living in Asia Minor. The old Greek historian explains that they are a class of Medes who left for greener pastures in Turkey. Herodotus does not really describe them as a religious order or an ethnic group; in fact, he paints a picture of refugees from Persia, Parthia, Bactria, Chorasmia (huh?) Aria (is that really a place), Media, Sakas, Samaria, Ethiopia, and Egypt. These people are kinda like the Pilgrims who created a melting pot of cultures. Remember, the early Christian Church does not thrive in the Holy Lands—it thrives in the Seven Churches, many of which were in…you guessed it, Asia Minor, home of the Magi 3.0.

Magi 4.0 have a very unique meaning. These Magi were religious authorities within the Persian court. They were educators with a specific purpose: educating the Emperor-to-be. In this light, how cool would the Magi 4.0 be if they were indeed teachers who offered their services to the King-of-all-Kings, baby Jesus.

So let's keep an open mind involving our Wise Men since there are a lot of possible historical meanings.

The Date of Arrival

Let's look at what Matthew wrote:

[Matthew 2:1] Now when Jesus was born in Bethlehem of Judaea in the days of Herod the king, behold, there came wise men from the east to Jerusalem, [2] Saying, Where is he that is born King of the Jews? for we have seen his star in the east, and are come to worship him.

How long after Jesus was born? Because it matters. If it was within the first eight days, then Jesus was in Bethlehem. If it was during days 9-39, then Jesus was with (Zacharias) in a house at (Bethany). If they came exactly on Day 40, then Jesus was in the same city, Jerusalem.

What about Nazareth? First of all, the town of Nazareth would have certainly taken notice of this visit, right? Second, Joseph leaves immediately after the Magi visit and hides from Herod. If the Magi visited Joseph's house in Nazareth, then he would have gone TOWARD Herod instead of away from danger in order to get to Egypt. If Nazareth, why not go to Asia Minor? Other problem with Nazareth is the tight window involving Herod. Notice how the passage clearly states "in the days of Herod the King"? Herod dies in March of 4 BC. Quirinius (the census guy) also arrives in Syria in 4 BC. While possible, a return trip to Nazareth, then a trip to Egypt, prior to March is a bit tight. I am not a fan of the Nazareth theory, nor am I a fan of a two-year-old Jesus.

I'll explain soon.

Place vs Direction

Now, pay close attention to what is actually written. Nowhere does it say the origins of the Magi. Yes, they came from the East. Yes, they saw the Star when they were in the East, but those details do not completely seal the deal. After all, why didn't they just say, "We saw the star when we were in Parthia?" Parthia was a major rival to Rome. Folks knew it well. There were highways leading right to the major cities. Unless…east meant someplace even farther than old Babylon (present Iraq/Iran). What if it was a country Herod didn't know?

Seen vs. Followed

Another thing to notice in the passage is that they did not claim to have followed it to Jerusalem. They claimed to have seen the "star" when they were in the East. That specific time and place. Back when they were in the East (wherever that was), they received some sort of sign/message and headed to Jerusalem because that is where the King of the Jews is supposed to be found. No wandering. No charting. No crossing deserts. They got the message, departed, and now wanted to see the prophecy fulfilled.

But, but…the star led them. Did it? How is this even possible? If anything, they saw the "star" in the eastern sky, which would have led them…east. But you can't follow a star because the earth is spinning on an axis. On any given time at night, a star, comet, or whatever would be seen in a different location because we are moving and it is fixed. Yes, it could help with some latitudinal/longitudinal navigating, but the line would have been infinite. The Wise Men would have just gone round and round the earth because the star never would have pinpointed a location on the globe.

Plot a Course to Jerusalem

In a few verses, they're going to get all excited when they see the "star" again, meaning they hadn't seen it since they left. They knew where to go: Jerusalem.

So does this mean they were Jewish? Or believers?

We're not told how much of a message this sign/omen gave them, and even if it was some convoluted astronomical alignment, they would have needed to be well-versed in God-lore for them to really care, right? They cared.

We do know, for certain, of their purpose: they want to worship Jesus. That's pretty cool. It also would be quite terrifying to King Herod.

[Matthew 2:3] When Herod the king had heard these things, he was troubled, and all Jerusalem with him.

Why would Herod even bother to meet with some Astromen? If he heard of their purpose, why not just send out some of his guards, arrest them, torture them, and get all of the details he needed? Instead, Matthew writes that "all Jerusalem" was troubled. Do you know what this means? Herod may have had this meeting in public. Really? Why would you have a public meeting with some religious fanatics? Isn't this something to do be-behind closed doors where you could deal with it in all sorts of shady ways.

Unless...(and it doesn't say it here)...these men were kings? Think about it, Herod had a choice Mediterranean kingdom, supported by the Romans, and had cleaned it up to be quite a vacation destination (don't picture later Israel). Why would this prima donna bother with these guys UNLESS they had an impressive entourage? Magi would be treated with disdain, but Kings would have been treated as equals.

Another way "all Jerusalem" would have been troubled is if two things were going on at once. Picture this, at the city gates, a large caravan of foreigners show up, declaring to Jewish/Roman guards that they wanted entrance to the city so they could see the "King of the Jews."

"You mean Herod? Sure, this way..."

Nope. Folks were troubled. So this might mean they were a bit more specific about the Christ rather than the King. While this bit of chaos is happening at the gates, think of what could be happening at the Temple. While the Pharisees are running to Herod to explain the meaning of the Wise Men's inquiry, Simeon and Anna are passing around the baby Jesus. Those who see this announcement would also throw fuel on the fire surrounding the arrival of the Wise Men.

Plus, wouldn't that be super cool if Jesus was actually in Jerusalem on Day 40 when the Wise Men arrived. Their Holy Spirit Radar was right. Jesus was in the city, but while they are meeting with Herod, Mary and Joseph meekly leave the city to go stay with (Zacharias) in a house in (Bethany).

The Wise Men also had a certain arrogance as well. Either in open court or in a public forum, they literally asked the people of Jerusalem where they could find Jesus. Dangerous, stupid, naïve…unless they came in force, under a foreign banner, and didn't sweat Herod. I know it doesn't say anything about them being kings (not here at least), but the behaviors exhibited do not lead me to believe they are foreign, pagan astronomers either.

The Pharisees Betray the Prophecy

[Matthew 2:4] And when he had gathered all the chief priests and scribes of the people together, he (Herod) demanded of them where Christ should be born. [5]And they said unto him, In Bethlehem of Judaea: for thus it is written by the prophet, 6And thou Bethlehem, in the land of Juda, art not the least among the princes of Juda: for out of thee shall come a Governor, that shall rule my people Israel."

What? They knew? See, this is why I thought that the "registration" ploy was an obvious plot to kill off the prophecy. A. You've now got a list of names. B. If it works, you'll get all of the Jews to show up dutifully. If we get the House of David, who needs to register the rest of the families/houses. Bethlehem was a trap because everybody knew this verse. Obviously, the wise men didn't know this detail or they would have gone to Bethlehem, but the Pharisees? The Chief Priests? Herod?

Time out for just a second. Wasn't Zacharias a high ranking guy? While the whole Annas/Caiaphas coup might not have happened yet, we do know Zacharias was the "unofficial" high priest and respected member of any sort of think tank. If he was asked by Herod, how would he respond? The truth, lie, or cover-up?

This is why I don't think Zacharias was from Bethlehem AND he'd been part of the circumcision at Day 8. Unlike all the other scholars, he knows the Christ has already been born. Herod and the others seem to indicate that the Christ was still in the future. Zacharias knows Jesus, Mary, and Joseph are NOT in Bethlehem, whether he was in the silent minority or vocal majority in response to Herod. Long before an angel warned Joseph in a dream, Zacharias most likely knew Herod was scheming.

For Bethlehem…the gig is up. The cat is out of the bag. (Send in the troops and kill 'em all, and while we're at it, poison the Wise Men also. Wait! Maybe we would do this a little more discreetly.) Herod instead devises a muh-ha-ha kind of plan. He knows the Wise Men are devout suckers, and if properly spied upon, they would do all the dirty work for him. So he uses them.

Date of Departure

[Matthew 2:7] Then Herod, when he had privily called the wise men, inquired of them diligently what time the star appeared. 8And he sent them to Bethlehem, and said, Go and search diligently for the young child; and when ye have found him, bring me word again, that I may come and worship him also.

Herod is clever. "Privately" keeps his hands clean. "Privately" keeps the Jews calm and the Pharisees out of the loop. Herod realizes that the Wise Men left because of the "star" appearance and have been on the move (just not following the star) since that day. By finding out this detail, Herod thinks he can discern how old the Christ child is. Did one of the Wise Men say something? I think so. Later, Herod will have anyone under the age of two killed. Why? If the Wise Men told him they saw the "star" two years ago, Herod would only have to kill heirs/threats under two instead of causing massive bloodshed.

Pause for a moment.

If the implicit answer was two years (just a guess), then why did it take these guys so long to get to Jerusalem? A camel can travel a hundred miles a day. Even if they cut across the Arabian desert (why?) they could make a trip from ancient Babylon to Jerusalem in just a few weeks. Two years? Something is a bit off. Either their journey was very complicated—or they came from a place much farther than Parthia.

(unpause)

<u>Herod's Trap</u>

Herod's also a big, fat liar. He has no intention of worshipping the child, but if the Wise Men were truly suckers, they would lead Herod's spies to the exact house. The noble citizens of Bethlehem might trust these guys instead of his own henchmen. Search! Although they had the town, no one knew where to find the baby. The Wise Men would not only do all the hard work but would also lead the spies right to the baby. Suckers!

The tone also shifted a bit. Herod sent them. They didn't just go…he sent them. Did they notice the change in tone from their host? Curious.

[Matthew 2:9] When they had heard the king, they departed; and, lo, the star, which they saw in the east, went before them,

till it came and stood over where the young child was. [10] When they saw the star, they rejoiced with exceeding great joy."

Let's slow these two verses down a bit because quite a bit happened. First, I would like to establish that Bethlehem is just six miles from Jerusalem. If there were just three Wise Men, then they could have reached Bethlehem in an hour or two (this seems unlikely).

If they had a huge entourage befitting foreign kings (likely), things would have taken a bit longer. They probably spent the night at Herod's Palace. The next morning, the entire entourage would prepare and begin down the road to Bethle-hem…watched! Very watched! First, what peasant wouldn't try to sell goods to these guys along the way, so that certainly crowds the road. Second, Herod SENT these guys so he could kill Jesus. This implies he had spies (Hey, where's Caiaphas the Monkey at? We need him). The Wise Men make a slow-moving, easy target to follow.

We need a second night.

We need it for the "departure" from Jerusalem to make sense, and we also need it for them to see any sort of "star." So this WAS a very slow moving caravan, wasn't it? Before anybody did any kneeling, the sun had to go down, which meant they took their time (which made sense if they suspected a trap).

To give themselves more time, they undoubtedly camped on the edge of Bethlehem. If they were truly naïve, they would have needed a base camp before they began searching door to door. If they were onto Herod's plan, then they purposely avoided any door knocking to give themselves time to think. Either way, they were camped outside of Jerusalem when the "star" incident happened.

Stars vs. Angels

First, look what excited them about the star: it was the first time they'd seen it since they saw it in the east (two years earlier). This was a sign/omen to get worked up about.

For this to work, however, they had to be sleeping outdoors instead of in a kingly tent (in December it snows in Israel). If you INSIST on a divine beam of light from a literal star, everybody and Herod's mother would have seen it. Why would God light up the sky with a beam of light when everybody needed secrecy.

Remember, it is past Day 40, so Jesus is almost certainly NOT in Bethlehem still. This star beam (unless properly focused like a magnifying glass on an ant) would also not identify a specific house. If it is a cosmic occurrence…YAY! (but now what?) It would not help them identify any of the houses in Bethlehem, would it?

For various reasons, I have to utterly reject "star" as any cosmic occurrence and instead accept it as a **malak**.

In just the context of the passage, the malak "went" and then "stood" so they knew specifically in which house to find Jesus. How does a star stand? An angel, however, can stand. It can lead. It can show up in a tent, reveal itself, and help the Wise Men sneak away from both their tents and Bethlehem in the dead of the night, and then lead them to a specific house in a specific town (Bethany). An angel could do this, a star could not.

Problems for "astrostar"

- **Saw it 1 time while in the east**

- **Thus, no tracking**
- **Thus, no guidance**
- **Thus, only announcing.**

Other problems for "astrostar"

- **It appears outside of Jerusalem to guide them to a house.**
- **Thus, not big/bright enough to attract Herod**
- **Thus, small enough to pinpoint**

Yet other issues for "astrostar"

- **It "moved" and "stood."**
- **Thus, it seems more than just light**

Precedents for "star" equaling an angel/malak:

- **Job 38= "morning stars sang" and "sons of God"**
- **Jude 13="Wandering stars" synonymous with Fallen angels**
- **Revelation 1= Seven stars are the seven archangels.**
- **Revelation 22= Bright morning star a reference for Jesus**
- **Revelation 2:28= Morning Star seems to be a title previously held by Lucifer/Satan**
- **Revelation 12=Stars of Heaven are the angels.**

Certainly, I could be wrong, but I just don't get what's going on if it was a beam of light. In a bit, Herod finds out he was tricked when the Wise Men bolt. If they went to Bethlehem, then it was a successful trap by Herod. If they didn't go to Bethlehem, Herod would know he was bamboozled, right? Why did he kill all the babies?

…Because the Wise Men vanished <u>before</u> going into Bethlehem.

Remember, God does NOT want Herod to find baby Jesus. Why would the angel be complicit in giving up this vital bit of information? I believe God sends a star-angel to redirect the Wise Men to another house in another town.

<u>A House in Bethany</u>

It should be a house that's hard to find. It should be a house from which it is easy to get back to the east. It should be a house that would allow safe passage to Egypt. It should also be reasonably close to Bethlehem but not be Jerusalem (since they had just "departed" Jerusalem).

Bethany fits most of those needs. Again, I'm not positive where Zacharias would live (Lazarus speculation only), but I have strong feelings where he would NOT live. How would he know if they bolted unless they didn't go to Bethlehem?

> **[Matthew 2:11] And when they were come into the house, they saw the young child with Mary his mother, and fell down, and worshipped him: and when they had opened their treasures, they presented unto him gifts; gold, and frankincense, and myrrh. [12] And being warned of God in a dream that they should not return to Herod, they departed into their own country another way.**

Another way? See, if this was Bethlehem, this is very problematic, but Bethany is on the eastern slope of the mountains/hills of Judea. From Bethany, it is a straight shot into the deserts. From Bethany, it is a straight shot south along the good side of the Dead Sea. Departing from Bethlehem or Jerusalem (and even worse, Nazareth) causes all sorts of schematic problems for the two sets of travelers. Did the Wise Men leave without their retinue of travelers, leaving the Jewish spies bewildered? Did the caravan break up into a hundred parts, like bugs scurrying away from the light?

When they DIDN'T go to Bethlehem, Herod and his spies knew they'd been bamboozled.

Before we deal with the treasures and the identities of the Wise Men, just remember that when Herod's spies wake up the next morning and the Wise Men are gone, he knows they tricked him.

The Treasure

Every time a Prophet opened his mouth, Satan chuckled. Remember the first Christ prophecy? All it said was the "seed of Eve," leaving Satan with a burning desire to wipe out humanity. Then it got specific. VERY specific. Each of these specific prophecies heaped more detail upon Christ promise, and also made it harder to fulfill. If you go back to Chapter Two, any of these prophecies left unfulfilled would have been a win for Satan. God had to bat 1.000 for the Christ to happen.

One of the strangest (and coolest) prophecies is an ancient tale about the treasures the Wise Men carried with them—Gold, (Frank)incense, and Myrrh. Get this…the treasures are re-gifted! Instead of stopping by the Toys for Tots store in Damascus, the Wise Men were caretakers of ancient gifts meant to be handed over to the Christ when he takes bodily form.

Now, any modern asterisk maker can point out the 1st century details about the treasures. Gold is, well, gold. It could have come from anywhere. The incense and myrrh, however, would have come from specific places (if you keep this story simple).

Frankincense most likely would have come from either the Arabian peninsula or from Somalia. It was so popular, that the infamous Silk Road connected to Africa to swap goods from ancient China. Rome helped this whole process by building good roads and bringing stability to the Middle East. There were now major highways for the Silk Road merchants. Myrrh also came from a specific source: Ethiopia.

Frankincense and myrrh had great value. Uses included perfumes, medicinal, eye shadow, embalming, wine mix, and even a cure for snakebite.

So while Mary and Joseph might have appreciated a baby blanket or diapers, these gifts were also nice.

Unless…

There are some Old Testament prophecies that seemed to predict the coming of the Wise Men, which is why I didn't dismiss this ancient story. It fits, despite the quality of its source.

Backstory for the Treasures

The "spurious" work I'm referencing is ***The Conflict of Adam and Eve with Satan***, which is often referred to as a "lost" book by the History Channel types. It is not credible. The Egyptian/Arabic author is unknown. It is a written account of a flawed oral tradition.

While none of it can be treated as "gospel," it introduces an idea that is not just curious but kinda awesome. Here's a recap of what A&E I Book XXX says:

Right after the Fall and Expulsion from the Garden, Satan was mad! In fact, A&E claims that Satan tried to kill Adam and Eve, which God would simply not allow. Adam and Eve were taken by two angels (Suriyel and Salathiel) to the Holy Mountain (see <u>Ezekiel 28:14</u>) where they could be safe from future attacks. On the Holy Mountain, there was a cave where the depressed couple could stay. For three days, Adam and Even stayed in this dark cave, mourning their fallen state. It was a tough transition from God's grace and the Garden.

To "cheer them up," God sent his angels on three specific tasks. He sent Michael to get some "golden rods," Gabriel to get some incense from the Garden, and Raphael brought myrrh that had been dipped and purified in a holy spring. After three days in the ground, Adam and Eve were presented with their present.

(See, even though this is a spurious book, it tells a nice story, doesn't it?)

Now this next section made my jaw drop, so I'll give you the translated lines word-for-word.

Book XXXI "For I shall come and save thee; and kings shall bring me when in the flesh, gold, incense, and myrrh; gold as a token of My kingdom, incense as a token of My divinity, and myrrh as a token of My suffering and My death."

Re-gifting, indeed!

For nine hundred years, Adam and Eve kept these treasures in the cave, letting it remind them of the Garden while the gold actually is described as lighting the cave. When Adam is on his death bed, he gathers up his family and gives them some instructions.

- They were to preserve his body because…
- A flood was coming (in a few centuries)

- Take his body with them on the Ark (what's an Ark?).
- Rebury his body "in the middle of the earth"
- "For the place where my body shall be laid is the middle of the earth; God shall come from thence and shall save our kindred."

Bet you didn't picture a coffin along with the giraffes sticking their heads out the window of the Ark, did you? We'll get back to this in Lesson Twelve.

Let's focus on the treasure.

A&E II Book VIII, v17: "Preserve this gold, this incense, and this myrrh, that God has given us for a sign; for in the days that are coming, a flood will overwhelm the whole creation. But those who shall go into the Ark shall take with them the gold, incense, and myrrh, with my body in the midst of the earth."

And here is the really strange ending:

"Then, after a long time, the city in which the gold, incense, and myrrh are found with my body shall be plundered. But when it is spoiled, the gold, incense, and myrrh shall be taken care of with the spoil that is kept; and naught of them shall perish, until the Word of God made man shall come; when kings shall take them, and shall offer to him."

According to this 6th Century A.D. legend, the Wise Men were prophesied four thousand years before they showed up. If true, this is an amazing story that almost came to a tragic end at the hands of Herod. It is a good thing that an angel helped both at the beginning and end of this story.

Implications of the Legend

I know this tale is a bit far-fetched and too good to be true, but let's just entertain the idea for a bit. Let's walk this through.

So the flood comes. Noah, Shem, Japheth, Ham, and their wives get on the ark with the animals, Adam's body, and the three treasures. The gold would light the Ark, and the incense would make it smell like the Garden of Eden. Raven, Dove, unload. It is at this point that the tale requires some specific action—to rebury Adam. All of this would be taking place in the Tower of Babel era. According to the story, Shem, Japheth, and Ham would have found a nice place for Adam and the treasures, only to have them stolen.

Knowing this ahead of time would have meant two probable reactions. First, you shrug and let God's grace guide the treasures into the hands of the Wise Men two thousand years later OR you keep some of the treasure. If each brother took a bit and also left the rest at Adam's tomb, then it would be really hard for Satan to stop this prophecy from coming true.

Old Testament Prophecies

Of course, this is just a silly theory, right? None of this is biblically supported. The Wise Men were from Persia, and the treasures were locally bought and meaningless, right?

> **[Micah 5:2] But thou, Bethlehem Ephratah, though thou be little among the thousands of Judah, yet out of thee shall he come forth unto me that is to be ruler in Israel; whose goings forth have been from of old, from everlasting.**

[3] Therefore will he give them up, until the time that she which travaileth hath brought forth: then the remnant of his brethren shall return unto the children of Israel.

Okay, so Micah called it. Bethlehem? Check. Birth? Check. Remnant? Hmm…what does that mean? The most obvious answer would be the lost northern tribes. I like this because it would allow the Wise Men to be Hebrew (instead of Jewish) which is why they even knew about the Christ promise. If we expand this even further, it could also reference all the way back to the Ark, when Japheth went toward Europe, Ham went toward Africa, and Shem went East (and Middle East). If all three had the treasures at the Ark, then perhaps this "return" of the "remnant" is a reunification of both Jew and Gentile.

[Psalm 72:9] They that dwell in the wilderness shall bow before him; and his enemies shall lick the dust. 10 The kings of Tarshish and of the isles shall bring presents: the kings of Sheba and Seba shall offer gifts. [11] Yea, all kings shall fall down before him: all nations shall serve him.

Most of Psalm 72 talks about a Messiah, Christ, or Redemptive King, but these two verses offer up some awesome details. First, notice the term "wilderness" which could mean both literal desert or just a far off distant land. How distant? Well, Tarshish is Spain, and they had a name for a country on the far side of the Mediterranean Sea. How far is this "wilderness" then? Wait…Spain! My Wise Man has been traveling for a while if he came from Spain. This guy would be the "Japheth" Wise Man since Genesis 10 connects him to the European countries.

Ham's descendants were African, which is why Sheba and Seba were mentioned. Remember, Psalm 72 was written LONG before Rome, the Silk Road, and even the dispersing of the northern tribes. This prophecy also seems to be a gathering of the sons of Noah instead of the sons of Jacob. Here is another:

[Psalm 68:29] Because of thy temple at Jerusalem shall kings bring presents unto thee. [30] Rebuke the company of spearmen, the multitude of the bulls, with the calves of the people, till every one submit himself with pieces of silver: scatter thou the people that delight in war. [31] Princes shall come out of Egypt; Ethiopia shall soon stretch out her hands unto God. [32] Sing unto God, ye kingdoms of the earth; O sing praises unto the Lord; Selah

Whether three kings or thirty, the gathering of the Wise Men must have been quite impressive, especially when you look at how Isaiah describes it:

[Isaiah 60:1] Arise, shine; for thy light is come, and the glory of the LORD is risen upon thee.[2] For, behold, the darkness shall cover the earth, and gross darkness the people: but the LORD shall arise upon thee, and his glory shall be seen upon thee. [3] And the Gentiles shall come to thy light, and kings to the brightness of thy rising. [4] Lift up thine eyes round about, and see: all they gather themselves together, they come to thee: thy sons shall come from far, and thy daughters shall be nursed at thy side. [5] Then thou shalt see, and flow together, and thine heart shall fear, and be enlarged; because the abundance of the sea shall be converted unto thee, the forces of the Gentiles shall come unto thee. [6] The multitude of camels shall cover thee, the dromedaries of Midian and Ephah; all they from Sheba shall come: they shall bring gold and incense; and they shall shew forth the praises of the LORD. [7] All the flocks of Kedar shall be gathered together unto thee, the rams of Nebaioth shall minister unto thee: they shall come up with

acceptance on mine altar, and I will glorify the house of my glory. [8] Who are these that fly as a cloud, and as the doves to their windows? [9] Surely the isles shall wait for me, and the ships of Tarshish first, to bring thy sons from far, their silver and their gold with them, unto the name of the LORD thy God, and to the Holy One of Israel, because he hath glorified thee.

Okay, now who's laughing at the A&E theory?

We have all three sons of Noah.

We have all three treasures.

We have the Christ.

We have camels!

This passage from Isaiah was written hundreds of years prior to the Wise Men. Unless it is an "End Times" prophecy, what else is it talking about other than the Wise Men? If this IS the Wise Men prophecy, then look at all of the wonderful details it describes and amplifies. The caravan that parks outside of Jerusalem is indeed quite massive. It is also an international coalition, which is why Jerusalem is described as being frightened and alarmed. This is also why it took a bit for them to bop on down to Bethlehem. A large coalition would also make it easy for the Wise Men to vanish from the midst of their retinue. However, if you match up all of these details with what is described in the Nativity story, then this coalition gathered together before marching for Jerusalem. Where did they gather? A king from Tarshish travels from the West. A king from Sheba travels from the south? Once they gathered, is that when the Angel appeared to them in the East? Did they glean the information to determine to go to Jerusalem or did the Angel "tell" them?

Legends of the Magi

So you now understand why I think all three sons of Noah were represented. The artistic renditions of the Three Kings as African, Asian, and Caucasian is actually not a modern invention but a very old interpretation dating back to the B.C. era.

Surprisingly, there is a lot of information about the identities of the Wise Men, but there is absolutely not consistency or common ground. The most commonly accepted identities comes from an Alexandrian document dated 500 AD which describes the three kings as Melchior, a Persian, Caspar, an Indian, and Balthazar, an Arabian.

Syrian Christians have a tradition of the Three Kings as being named Larvandad, Gushnasaph, and Hormisdas.

Huh?

Ethiopian Christians (remember the Psalms about Ethiopia) name the kings as Hor, Karsudan, and Basanater.

Armenia, which is where Mount Ararat/Ark is located, lists Kagpha, Badadakharida, and Badadilma as the three kings.

If Isaiah 60 is accurate, it could be that all of these traditions are correct and there were simply a dozen or more kings in the coalition.

There is an endearing tale about Jesus and an eastern king by the name of Gondophares. According to the legend I read, this king sent an envoy to Jesus during the days of his ministry (not recorded in the Gospels). Jesus politely told the envoy that he had little time to do his work, but later, they would send a disciple to bring the Gospel to the king. After the Crucifixion, this task fell to Thomas, who went way out to present day Kandahar (later Thomas died in India=ambition!). What intrigues me is what a king as far as Afghanistan was doing sending letters to Jesus? How did he even know of a Messiah unless...

We Three Kings of Orient are...

There is another tale from ancient Taxila (in Pakistan) that the Wise Men passed by while taking the Silk Road (that led to China). How far "east" is east?" Well, let's look at a disjointed piece of history that does not fit anything except the Wise Men theory. In 1243, a Christian named Prester John was sent to meet the Kublai Khan in China. He reported that the whole land of "Chata" were believers that traced their heritage back through a Mongol line that claimed to have descended from the original Magi. These people (the Naimans) hailed from central Asia.

If a Wise Man-Magi-King did come face-to-face with baby Jesus, he would not be able to go back to the gods of his fathers, but would preach and teach a limited Gospel to all those around him. After 1,200 years, a bit of it remained for Prester John to discover.

Marco Polo also mentioned that he saw the tombs of a Wise Man-Magi-King during his visit in Saba, Iran.

St. Helena used the might of her son's Roman Empire to track down the remains of the Wise Men and gather them at a shrine in Constantinople while Cologne, Germany believes it has the remains of the three kings.

Departing (Bethany)

Now, to fulfill the prophecy, Herod had to be tricked. This coalition of kings knew they were being watched, and whether the star-angel led them away, or they snuck out and THEN saw the star-angel, they mostly likely could not bring their whole posse with them. Luke seems to indicate that on the same night they gave the treasures they also learned they needed to vanish by morning. Herod's spies, still sitting outside of Bethlehem, must have been quite surprised when this international coalition scattered without going to Bethlehem or returning to Jerusalem.

Let's stay in (Bethany) for a bit. Let's imagine the Wise Men (kings) presenting their treasures to baby Jesus, Mary, and Joseph. Is Elizabeth, Zacharias, and baby John in your imagination? Are they there? Are there other people from (Bethany) also there? More likely than not, the visiting (kings) could not speak with the inhabitants of the house. How do they relay the harrowing journey the treasures had just taken?

The hostess would have fed them and given them a place to sleep, but by the next morning, they were gone. These three kings or thirty magi, or three hundred wise men would all go back to their countries, nourished and ready to receive the full Gospel by the end of the next generation. Wherever they went, they or their children would have been ready converts to Christianity.

Did Joseph have his dream on the same night? While it is possible some time went by, Herod would have been looking for answers. Letting Joseph linger for a few more days seems unlikely. I think both warnings happened that night.

So by morning in (Bethany), everyone is scattering while spies are running back to Jerusalem to tell Herod about what was happening (nothing) in Bethlehem. What happens to the treasure?

There are all sorts of theories about the treasures.

One story tells a tale that the two thieves on Calvary stole the gold years earlier.

Another tale says that little Judas absconded it.

The most popular tale is that Mary and Joseph used it to finance their trip to Egypt.

The Last Magi

However, I'd like to throw out another theory: Mary Magdalene. Now, I'm not going to argue the difference between Mary Magdalene and Mary of Bethany right here (I'll save that for my Imagining Easter book). If the two Marys are one and the same, then Mary Magdalene was a prostitute who was born in Bethany and was found possessed by seven demons near Magdala (Lake Galilee). If the same person, then it is no wonder Martha is so judgmental of her tarnished sister.

In John 12, we read the end of a 4,000-year-old story. Do a little digging, and you will learn that the value of the alabaster box was the equivalence to a full year's worth of wages. What prostitute would hold onto such a thing? Unless it was as precious as her soul.

My speculation is that in the town of Bethany in the year 4 BC, there was a family near to Zacharias and Elizabeth. This family had three children, Mary, Martha, and Lazarus (who most likely was not born yet or was older than 2). This family knew the secret of the Wise Men, baby John, and baby Jesus. They could be trusted. Years later, Mary and Joseph returned to this family for hospitality during the three annual festivals, which is why Jesus and Lazarus became close friends.

Mary? She must've been a bit older, and although I have no clue how she strayed so far, Jesus went and found her at Magdala and brought her back into the light. As the eldest daughter of Neighbor Bob, she had access to the spikenard and the incense.

Mary became the Last Magi.

Her task?

First, she anointed the Paschal Lamb prior to it being brought into the house with oil so valuable Satan (err, Judas), could not believe it still existed. While it is not clear if this spikenard was one of the Holy Treasures, a short time later, Mary is given a final task—preparing Jesus's body for the grave. What did she do? She wrapped him in a HUNDRED POUNDS of incense. Why? I believe it was the last of the Cave of Treasures incense, created with a promise that it would be used **"as a token of my suffering and death."**

CHAPTER TWELVE

OUT OF AFRICA

Unfortunately, we left off at Bethlehem, where Herod and his spies were quickly learning that the Wise Men wised up to his plan. Herod's Plan A (darn Varus) had been to get a name list of David heirs, which he could use to eliminate as many threats as he needed. Plan B was to have the Wise Men lead him directly to the Christ Child. Now that both plans have failed, Herod is left with an awful Plan C. If his spies had been able to pinpoint a specific house, it would have been over in just a few slashes of a sword. Believing the Christ child to be in Bethlehem, he overwhelms the little village with armed soldiers.

[Matthew 2:16] Then Herod, when he saw that he was mocked of the wise men, was exceeding wroth, and sent forth, and slew all the children that were in Bethlehem, and in all the coasts thereof, from two years old and under, according to the time which he had diligently inquired of the wise men. [17] Then was fulfilled that which was spoken by Jeremy (Jeremiah) the prophet, saying,

**[18] In Rama was there a voice heard, lamentation, and
weeping, and great mourning, Rachel weeping for her
children, and would not be comforted, because they are not.**

While the focus of this passage is all about Bethlehem, it
should be noted that the order extended to **"all the coasts"** of
Judea. Now, controlling the "media" reports for one small village is easy, but if Herod extended it beyond the town, then he
must have worried that the Christ escaped. History most likely
would have recorded a nation wide infanticide, so Herod must
have used specialized assassins to seek out specific situations.

Avoiding the Main Roads

This is why Mary and Joseph immediately had to leave the
country:

**[Matthew 2:13] And when they (the Wise Men) were departed,
behold, the angel of the Lord appeareth to Joseph in a dream,
saying, Arise, and take the young child and his mother, and
flee into Egypt, and be thou there until I bring thee word: for
Herod will seek the young child to destroy him.
[14] When he arose, he took the young child and his mother by
night, and departed into Egypt**

The route to Egypt is curious. If Herod was scouring the
coastlines, that meant that Mary and Joseph were not safe on the
"King's Highway" leading into Egypt. This international trade
route would have been monitored. I believe that Mary and Joseph were staying in Bethany, which was on the eastern side of
the mountains, and if they followed the shore of the Dead Sea,
they could have taken the "backwoods" route all the way to Ae-
ala, now the Port of Aqaba.

All of this is speculation. Maybe Joseph pulled an Obi Wan at each checkpoint (You don't need to see our papers. This isn't the baby you're looking for. Go about your business). Could be? However, if Joseph were cautious, he and Mary would have taken the safer passage out of Judea. Perhaps they had Wise Men to help them? They certainly could buy their passage. While it is possible that they walked to Egypt, I LOVE the idea of Jesus re-crossing the Red Sea like Moses in reverse.

Where were they going?

If Herod was searching the highways along the coast, then he might have been so bold as to extend his reach into the delta region that later became Cairo. This works if Mary and Joseph walked. If they took a boat ride across the Red Sea, they would have entered Egypt anywhere south of Herod's spies.

Mary and Joseph had no idea how long they were going to hide in Egypt. All they knew was that they needed to avoid this psychopathic killer hunting for Jesus. So where did they stay? Who knows?

The Red Pyramid Theory

So what did Shem, Japheth, and Ham do with the body of Adam? In the text of A&EII, Book VIII, they were tasked with placing his body in the "middle of the earth" because "God shall come from thence and shall save our kindred." Does this sound familiar? This is what Matthew wrote:

> **[Matthew 2:15] And was there until the death of Herod: that it might be fulfilled which was spoken of the Lord by the prophet, saying, Out of Egypt have I called my son.**

Is Matthew referencing Hosea or an older prophecy? Regardless, the angel set the trip into motion BECAUSE of a prophecy, so I needed to find a place where they could go with some meaning.

Having studied the Great Pyramid in Giza, I knew all about its astronomical significance along with its strange lack of hieroglyphics. According to Pharaoh's official history, it was made for Khufu and certainly not a dead man named Adam. The Great Pyramid was looted of treasure and bodies. Double check.

However, a few miles south, there is an even cooler pyramid, the Red Pyramid. It was the FIRST true smooth sided pyramid built of red limestone. Adam, according to Josephus, was coincidentally formed of 'red earth," matching some nice symbolism. It was built for Sneferu (not to be confused with Adam) but the date of 2600 BC matches pretty close to the same estimation for the Great Flood. Egyptologists say it was built with tricks and traps to keep its contents from grave robbers. It was built with only one burial chamber, and the mummy placed there was also removed. A wall was also built around it.

Curious.

While Coptic traditions list a bunch of possible locations where Mary and Joseph stayed while in Egypt, I read an article about how the Christians living in Dahshur (right next to the Red Pyramid) claimed to celebrate the specific location where they stayed. I read about this because the entire Christian population had to flee for their lives during recent persecution. I think there would be some lovely symbolism if Jesus went to the place Adam and the treasures had possibly been kept.

[Matthew 2:19] But when Herod was dead, behold, an angel of the Lord appeareth in a dream to Joseph in Egypt, [20] Saying, Arise, and take the young child and his mother, and go into the land of Israel: for they are dead which sought the young child's life.[21] And he arose, and took the young child and his mother, and came into the land of Israel. [22] But when he heard that Archelaus did reign in Judaea in the room of his father Herod, he was afraid to go thither: notwithstanding, being warned of God in a dream, he turned aside into the parts of Galilee: [23] And he came and dwelt in a city called Nazareth: that it might be fulfilled which was spoken by the prophets, He shall be called a Nazarene.

According to some historians, Herod died only a few months after the Slaughter of the Innocents, meaning Mary and Joseph only had to stay in a foreign country for a few months. Other historians debate the death of Herod, but three months or three years really don't matter. Jesus went back to Nazareth.

But that wraps up the Nativity Story.

I hope you enjoyed a tour inside of my head, because this is the sort of stuff that fills my thoughts while everyone else is singing "Jingle Bells."

If I'm wrong (and you **know** it), then I hope your resolve strengthens your faith. There are so many fascinating moments in the Nativity story, and I hope I gave you something to think about.

ABOUT THE AUTHOR

Jason Lee Willis, a self-described Luth-olic-a-tist, characterizes himself as "just a nerd with a Bible" and has led adult and youth small group studies at home and at church for the past three decades. As a former English teacher who explored literature to find possibilities rather than absolute answers, Willis looks for "out of the box" interpretations with a preference for the most "epic" answers. While versed in world mythology and history, he remains the son of the church secretary raised in a conservative small town.

ALSO BY JASON LEE WILLIS
Examining the Beloved Disciple
Examining Moses
Examining Gospel Timelines
Examining the Seven Kings

www.ingramcontent.com/pod-product-compliance
Lightning Source LLC
Chambersburg PA
CBHW060409310726
48976CB00003B/994